KU-698-347

Forever
Is
TRUE

BY THE SAME AUTHOR

A Thing beyond Forever
That Kiss in the Rain
How about a Sin Tonight?
Ex
Black Suits You
Forever Is a Lie

Stranger Trilogy
Marry Me, Stranger
All Yours, Stranger
Forget Me Not, Stranger

Forever Is TRUE

NOVONEEL CHAKRABORTY

EBURY
PRESS

An imprint of Penguin Random House

EBURY PRESS

USA | Canada | UK | Ireland | Australia
New Zealand | India | South Africa | China

Ebury Press is part of the Penguin Random House group of companies
whose addresses can be found at global.penguinrandomhouse.com

Published by Penguin Random House India Pvt. Ltd
7th Floor, Infinity Tower C, DLF Cyber City,
Gurgaon 122 002, Haryana, India

First published in Ebury Press by Penguin Random House India 2017

Copyright © Novoneel Chakraborty 2017

All rights reserved

10 9 8 7 6 5 4 3 2 1

This is a work of fiction. Names, characters, places and incidents are either the
product of the author's imagination or are used fictitiously and any resemblance
to any actual person, living or dead, events or locales is entirely coincidental.

ISBN 9780143427506

Typeset in Requiem Text by Manipal Digital Systems, Manipal
Printed at Thomson Press India Ltd, New Delhi

This book is sold subject to the condition that it shall not, by way of trade
or otherwise, be lent, resold, hired out, or otherwise circulated without the
publisher's prior consent in any form of binding or cover other than that in
which it is published and without a similar condition including this condition
being imposed on the subsequent purchaser.

www.penguin.co.in

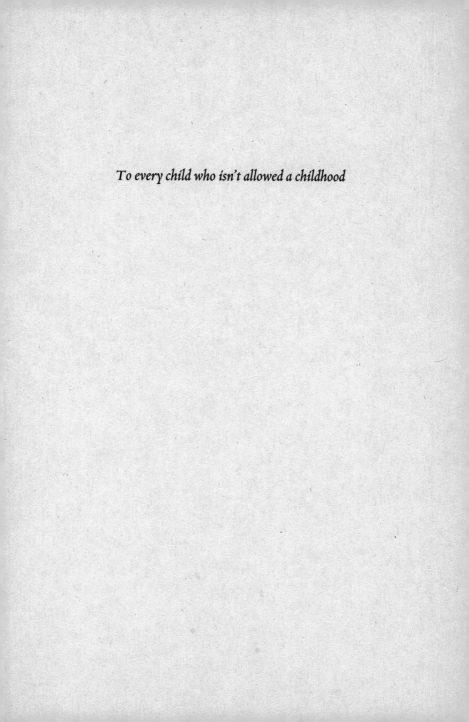

To every child who isn't allowed a childhood

Prologue

'I'm sorry, Prisha, but I had no other option,' the person said, standing close to the hospital bed on which Prisha was lying with her eyes closed. Beneath a blanket that covered her till her bosom, she was wearing a sky-blue patient's uniform. Her forehead was freshly bandaged. Her right hand, with a drip, was placed on her belly while the left one was by her side, a pulse-monitoring clip attached to the index finger. There was a saline water stand beside the bed. Her left leg was plastered and her face bruised. It was quiet except for the occasional beeping of the monitor that was keeping a track of her heartbeats. The room was bathed in an eerie green-coloured light.

'Just like I had no other option with Ishanvi. She was a good girl. So were you. But you both fell for the wrong person, bad person. And sometimes, even when you aren't at fault, life still holds you guilty and makes you pay for it. But how do you atone for something you haven't done?' Silence. The person grasped Prisha's left hand. It was cold.

'Not that I expected you to be alive but now I can at least talk to you, unlike Ishanvi.'

After a deep sigh, the person added, 'I had tried warning you like I had tried warning Ishanvi but neither of you paid heed. Why? You were in love. *Love!* I hate that emotion because it is the most customizable emotion a human can feel. Its definition changes the way one thinks. Its syntax changes the way one feels. It is not like sadness or happiness. It is not absolute. Though we think it is. I hate it. In fact, hate is a soft word. I abhor love, loathe it. If you had been in your senses, I'm sure you would have asked what makes me so anti love. Well, it is a long story but I carry the moral in my heart every day. And will do so till I turn into ashes.'

There was silence. The person caressed Prisha's forehead.

'Unfortunately, nobody will ever know my story. But that doesn't bother me. The only thing that bothers me is that the person who mattered the most to me will also never get to hear my story. You tell me, Prisha, is it fair to live someone else's story all your life? But . . . ' The person leaned close to her left ear and whispered, 'If you can listen, then listen well. Chances are you will die soon on this bed. But in case you survive, don't push me into killing you again. Next time, there won't be any passerby to bring you to any hospital on time. One last request: don't test me for I've been killing people for a long time now. You are my only failure. And failing is something which doesn't go down well with me.' After staring at Prisha for a while, the person said, 'May your soul rest in peace, Prisha. Next life, choose someone better. Choose someone who's worth it.'

The person stopped caressing her forehead and tiptoed out of the room. Prisha had opened her eyes by then. She had been in her senses throughout. *Or was she?* She didn't see the person's face but she did feel the person's touch. Contrary to the person's words, the touch wasn't threatening. The last statement had made her hair stand on its end.

This was the first time Saveer had visited her in the hospital since she had regained consciousness. *Why would he want to kill her?* she wondered. *Or for that matter Ishanvi?* These, however, were the least of her concerns at that moment. There was something she noticed that was extremely disturbing. Prisha saw the person leaving the room. But in a woman's attire.

What's wrong with Saveer? she wondered. Then she thought to herself: *was she hallucinating because of the heavy sedatives she had been taking for some time now?* Prisha couldn't tell. She dozed off.

1

Six months later . . .

The inners, the shirt and the trousers that her parents had brought for her fitted her perfectly. The clothes were old but after wearing them, she felt new. Two months ago, when Prisha had seen herself in the hospital's washroom mirror, she had thought that she would never regain what she had lost in that fall. Oh, it wasn't a wilful fall. It was a push. A deliberate push. And with it, she hadn't just lost herself but a lot more.

It was Gauri who had told her how she had been found and admitted to the hospital. She herself had heard half the story from the couple who had found Prisha and the other half from Saveer, who had rushed her to Fortis Hospital. After a search that lasted for six hours, Prisha's body was found stuck between three rocks. Her dress was torn from behind. Her face was smeared with blood. There was a deep gash on her left eyebrow and her right leg was badly injured.

Prisha was discovered through a selfie taken by a couple who had also gone to Nandi Hills that morning. The picture was a high-angle shot taken close to the edge of the cliff with the couple in the foreground and the abyss in the background. The couple noticed something untoward in the background while looking at the photo. They magnified the image and realized that a person seemed to be stuck between the jagged rocks. They immediately called up the police. By the time the cops arrived, Saveer had also reached the accident spot.

Prisha was extricated using a crane. Saveer stood shivering on the hill. He felt his heart slowing down even though in reality it was beating furiously. When the crane pulled Prisha out and placed her on the ground, he froze. He was waiting for someone to confirm that she was alive. The doctor with the search party announced that her heart was beating even though she was unconscious. Prisha was placed on a stretcher and carried inside an ambulance. Watching the retreating vehicle in the distance, Saveer finally managed to find his voice. He called up Gauri and asked her to reach Fortis Hospital.

Gauri and Diggy, clueless and nervous, met Saveer in the hospital lobby. He briefed them on the accident.

'But how did she fall off the cliff?' Gauri asked, incredulous.

'I don't know,' Saveer said and continued after a thoughtful pause, 'She'd asked me to meet her at Nandi

Hills. It is my birthday so I thought she must have planned something. By the time I reached there, there were cops, a search team and the family that had spotted her.'

Since then, Prisha was told, Saveer had visited the hospital every single day for six months during visiting hours, sat in the lobby for as long as a visitor was allowed to and then went back home. Gauri had told Saveer to meet Prisha innumerable times. But he didn't. He had asked Gauri to tell Prisha that he had never visited the hospital. No reasons cited. But now that it was the day of her discharge, Gauri thought Prisha should know the truth. But Prisha could only think of one thing once Gauri had told her everything: Saveer did visit her. In a woman's dress. *Who was he hiding from?* she wondered.

While Gauri and Prisha were talking, Mrs Srivastav entered the room and slid a pearl-studded silver ring on Prisha's finger. She had consulted an astrologer, who had advised that Prisha should wear the ring the moment she was released from the hospital as a safeguard against any further accidents. The one she had survived was supposedly in her *kundali*. Though Prisha didn't believe in astrology, she nonetheless wore the ring without any fuss. She had seen how her parents had been shuttling back and forth between Delhi and Bengaluru for the last six months. While her mother, Anupriya Srivastav, had moved to Bengaluru—she stayed at a hotel for a few days and then later shifted in with Zinnia—her father, Ashok Srivastav, and her younger sister, Ayushee, visited her every weekend. Their plan was simple. Once Prisha recuperated, they would bring her back to Faridabad with them. And today was the day.

For the first time in six months, Prisha felt the rays of the sun kiss her skin the moment she stepped out of the hospital. For her parents, for Gauri and Diggy, for Zinnia, and for the nurses, who had now become acquaintances, she was finally free. But she knew there were a lot of questions that she needed answers to. The first being: why did Saveer push her? She loved him. Even he loved her. Or had said so. But his eyes . . . every time he had told her that he loved her . . . his eyes spoke of genuineness. The way he had made love to her couldn't have been just lust. The way he . . . Lying on the hospital bed for the past six months, Prisha had fought only one fierce inner battle: against herself. The result: she had a gut feeling that Saveer hadn't pushed her.

'Now don't be so quiet,' Mrs Srivastav said. 'By god's grace, you're completely fine now. Accidents happen but they won't happen again.' She caressed Prisha's forehead. They were on their way back from the hospital in a cab. Prisha, her mother and Zinnia were sitting behind while Gauri was sitting beside the driver. Her father, sister and Diggy were following them in another cab.

Gauri said, 'I wanted to ask you this since day one but then your condition was such that . . . anyway . . . I really want to know how you fell off the cliff?'

There was a momentary silence.

'Yes, what happened?' Zinnia said, turning to face Prisha. Mrs Srivastav too looked at her daughter expectantly.

The wait for Saveer at the edge of the hill . . . her constant attempt at perfecting those words in Kannada . . . just for him . . . someone's appearance . . . the person's apology . . . the push . . . and the fall. Everything flashed in front of Prisha. She still thought that someone would tell her it hadn't happened. That it was all a bad dream.

'We are waiting,' Gauri urged.

'I slipped,' Prisha said. She didn't wait to see their reactions. She turned to look out of the window. *No tears,* she told herself.

2

He was doing the last set of shoulder push-ups—legs against a wall and head facing the floor, beads of perspiration on his forehead. It was morning and he was on the terrace of his house.

Saveer knew which day it was: the one he had been waiting for a long time. The day Prisha was going to be discharged from the hospital. When the search team had pulled her out, something had told him that he won't find her looking at him again. He won't hear his name from her lips again. And he won't feel her lips on him again, telling him that forever is, perhaps, true.

Done with the push-ups, Saveer took a break and sat down on the floor, his heart racing, struggling to stabilize. He looked at his reflection in an old mirror in front of him. He could see a man who wanted to love but was not destined to. With locked jaws, he stood up and walked towards the mirror. He took off his gym vest and turned his back to the mirror and craned his neck to read it for the umpteenth time in the last six months: *I will fuck your every happiness.*

Saveer had no idea who had tattooed it on his back. And when. It was so weird to wake up one day and see those words tattooed on his back. Unless it had been there before, and he had never realized it. *That's weirder*, he thought. He had rarely looked in the mirror before. But that was beside the point now. He had no enemies. He didn't even have friends for that matter. *What did it mean?* Did the answer lay behind the truth that he had hidden from Ishanvi and Prisha? He had consulted the police as well but there was no lead beyond those six words. The police agreed to lodge a complaint if something else happened. Except for frustration on Saveer's part, nothing else had happened. The fact that Prisha fell off the cliff, that too on his birthday, wasn't a coincidence. Ishanvi too was killed on his birthday. His brother, his dog, his first crush, everyone had died on his birthday. And all these deaths were such that there were no leads. That's why it had always seemed to him that perhaps they were a coincidence. That's why he had grown up believing what his mother had once said: that he was cursed. *Whoever loved him, died*. As he grew up and following the deaths of his loved ones, Saveer's belief only grew stronger: *I'll kill the ones who love me.*

It was twenty-five years since his brother, Veer Rathod, had died. Saveer was ten years old at that time. It was the first death in his family. And it was on his birthday: the beginning of the trend. Saveer's train of thoughts was interrupted as an alarm went off. He had set it himself. It was time for him to take a shower and leave. Prisha would be discharged from the hospital in a few hours.

Three hours later, Saveer was in his Audi, which was parked close to the hospital's exit. His eyes were fixed on the gate. He had seen Gauri, Diggy, Zinnia and Prisha's parents enter the main gate an hour and a half ago. After forty more minutes of impatient waiting, he spotted them coming out of the hospital. He wanted to reach out to Prisha and kiss her red. Hug her tightly. And dare anyone who thought they could be separated. His fingers tightened around the car's steering wheel. He relaxed his grip only when the group left the hospital. Saveer started following Prisha's cab.

He maintained a safe distance from the cab and thought that he wouldn't meet Prisha again. If at all their love story had to continue, then it would be a silent one. She had all the reasons to hate him. Especially if and when she learnt about what he had hidden from her. Not that he hadn't tried to decode the tattoo, reach a conclusion and eliminate it in order to weed out the fear that Prisha maybe snatched from him again. But nothing had worked out. And seeing Prisha walk out of the hospital, Saveer thought that it was too much of a risk to involve her again. It would also be selfish on his part knowing that there was someone behind the accidents. Until he was sure who had tattooed the line on his back, he wouldn't meet Prisha. Just that he was itching to know how she had fallen off the cliff. That could possibly give him a clue. Her falling off and him discovering the tattoo on his back on the same morning could not have been a coincidence. But when and how he would get to know the reason behind the fall was something he wasn't sure of. Saveer took a turn as he saw Prisha getting down from the car in front of Zinnia's apartment.

Sitting at the dining table at home that night and staring at the protein salad in front of him, Saveer prayed that Prisha wouldn't try to reach out to him. He wouldn't be able to face her and tell her the truth. *How can a series of deaths in the family be related to a single person?* Unless he himself was killing them. Nobody would believe him. In fact, it would not be uncommon for people to dismiss Saveer's claim as mere superstition. But only Saveer knew it was anything but superstition. It had happened for far too long and for far too many times to be a coincidence any more. And Prisha was the only one who had survived. But . . . what could it be if it wasn't a coincidence . . . if not a curse?

Saveer finished his dinner with a clogged mind. He went to his room, lay down on the bed and tried to think about it. By now, he knew only his memory could lead him to any possible clues. Why did Ishanvi die? Why did Prisha fall off the cliff? And whether his love story with Prisha too had reached its expiry date? He closed his eyes . . . and the first thing that flashed in front of him was the cute face of a young girl . . . Aditri . . . his first crush.

* * *

From Saveer's memory
His crush
1996

I remember it was on the first day of Class IX when I saw her for the first time. It was during the morning assembly. She was a newcomer asking around for her class' assembly line. I intentionally approached her, offering help. Everybody's eyes were shut during the prayer but mine were open. And they were on her. When I think about it now, it seems funny, but back then she had suddenly become extremely important for me. In just one glance, Aditri Agarwal had snuffed out all my other priorities.

She had bewitched me. It felt as if I went to school not to study but to see her. Since she was in a different section, we never really talked unless I intentionally asked her random questions if I saw her in the common corridor or next to the water cooler or in the canteen. But such occasions were rare. On those rare occasions, though, I discovered an even rarer satisfaction. I named it love. You know the kind that happens when you know nothing about anything but feel that you know a lot about everything? The kind that happens for the first time?

Initially, it seemed as if Aditri wasn't easy to impress. I would give her that obvious kind of attention in school, and later on in the coaching class as well, that a boy would give when he was in love. But she didn't seem to understand anything. Meanwhile, I started receiving paper chits in school with adjectives written on them like cute, handsome, irresistible, and what not. They kept me awake more than trigonometry and chemistry (the subjects I hated the most). And with every passing day, the number of chits kept increasing. I tried my best to catch the person behind them but couldn't. It was only when I decided to complain about it to the principal that I ran into Aditri right outside the headmistress' office. She asked me where I was going. I told her someone was constantly giving me chits and I didn't know what to do about it.

'And someone is constantly trying to impress me. I too don't know what to do about it.' Those were her exact words, I remember. An awkward silence fell between us. Then I knew why I shouldn't complain to the principal. It was Aditri who had been sending me those chits. She liked me as much as I liked her. But she was an introvert unlike me and thus got a kick out of seeing me getting all worked up after reading those chits.

I really won't ever be able to tell or write about what I felt in those days that followed with Aditri and me getting into a relationship. It was a first for both of us. There were so many times I felt that everything was unreal. I hugged her only to convince myself that I wasn't simply daydreaming. I introduced her to my best friend, to my family (not as a girlfriend but as a close friend). On weekdays, we would be together in school while during weekends, we were either at her or my place studying together. Our academic performance also got better unlike my other friends, who fared badly because they were in 'love'.

The best part about those days was that I wasn't emotionally corrupt. I strongly believed that my search for my soulmate had come to an end with Aditri. Her birthday was a month before mine. I remember sneaking out of my house an hour before midnight with my music system on my ranger cycle. I pedalled to her house and played the birthday song exactly at midnight. The inspiration was obvious: the character of Lloyd played by John Cusack from the movie *Say Anything*. It was my favourite movie at that time. Before her parents or the guard of her building could catch me, I sped away on the bicycle. The music system was left behind to keep playing the birthday song. Only Aditri knew it was mine. And that was what I cared about the most. The next day she thanked me by kissing me on my lips. She pressed her lips against mine for a microsecond but I felt the reverberations for a long, long time. I was waiting for the month to get over. I had planned to thank her on my birthday, her way.

My parents always had a small party at home on my birthday. It was embarrassing because there had been accidents in my family, twice, on my birthday— my brother's death and my uncle's sudden paralysis— and since then I had always felt weird celebrating my birthday. That year, of course, was special. Apart from my birthday, I had something else to look forward to. I had invited Aditri and her parents. She had called me to inform that her parents would come later since her father had some official work. I couldn't care less.

Aditri was supposed to come early in the evening. Around 5 p.m. But she didn't. Not even till 7 p.m. I called her landline many times. But there was no answer. In fact, when her parents arrived at around 8 p.m., I felt the first knot of fear in my stomach. They thought Aditri was already at my place. Her mother had gone to the market and was later picked up by her father. So there was nobody at home to answer my phone calls. Aditri's father called up the police. A search party was formed and the area from Aditri's house to mine scoured. Other students of our batch were contacted. Her parents were crying. And so was I. After around three–four hours, Aditri's body was found under an out-of-order lamp post in a lane next to my house. I wasn't allowed to see the body. The description which I overheard later had scarred me for a pretty long time. She had died from a traumatic head injury, haemorrhage from a scalp laceration. It was said that her long hair had somehow got entangled in the spokes of the back tyre of her bicycle, which led to her death. It was a freak accident. People tried to question it. I was one of them. But there was no alternative theory that we could come up with. And to this day, nobody knows for sure if it was an unfortunate accident or a . . . planned murder.

3

The thought of Aditri's body made Saveer sit up in bed. He had never seen the body, but had imagined it many a time. And the image had haunted him for as long as he could remember. So many deaths on his birthday. Prima facie, all of them seemed random. But until there was anything to prove otherwise, he would have to rely on coincidence. The tattoo was a clue. But it was a clue to a dead end. It was as if the person behind the deaths was telling Saveer, 'I wanted you to know my intention but not me.'

Saveer got out of bed. Sleep was nowhere on the horizon. He felt an urge to call up Prisha. He picked up his phone, scrolled down to her name and was about to tap on it when an impulse made him throw the phone on the bed. *I won't call her*, he sounded strict. He repeated the same to himself aloud a few more times to accept her absence.

There was a beep. He glanced at the mobile. There was another beep. Saveer realized the sound wasn't coming from the phone on the bed. It was the other phone, which he kept on the side table in the room. It was a new phone with an old number that he had recently reactivated. It was Mean Monster's number.

Prisha had been an emotional interlude for him. A much-needed one. An interlude that he had thought would finally bring him to his redemption. That through Prisha he would realize that the fear which he had harboured since childhood—anyone he loved would die, would turn out to be a thought-bubble. But it was not to be. He was happy that Prisha was still alive unlike the others. And he had no business taking another shot at togetherness, doesn't matter how much he itched to. What Ishanvi's death had taught him was actually the truth: perhaps he deserved all this. And till the time he didn't know why he deserved all this he would be better off punishing himself the way he had been till he'd met Prisha.

Saveer read the message on Tinder. Before Prisha, the Mean Monster only had to text his contacts that he was 'available', and requests would pour in. And with every girl, he got fresh pings. After all, what the Mean Monster did, few guys could: give women unprecedented orgasms by pushing them to their innermost sexual edge.

After staying away from the hook-up scene for nearly a year, he reluctantly downloaded Tinder and made some random swipes to reinitiate his emotional destruction.

Hi, this is Asmita. I've heard a lot about you from a friend months back. Are you really the Mean Monster or an imposter?

I'm the one. Saveer replied. He was breathing heavily.

How can I be sure? she asked.

There's only one way to know.

And what's that?

Try me.

Saveer hated himself for writing it. After a long time, he was back to hating himself. Back to the life he never thought he would live again. Especially after meeting Prisha. After falling in an impossible love with her.

Fair enough. The Sugar Factory @11 tonight?

Okay. I'll be next to the bar.

Like always, Saveer took a corner seat in The Sugar Factory, where his presence would be unassuming. He was trying hard not to think about anything. Thoughts would make him weak, make him crave for Prisha, make him want to meet her, even if it was just once. While Saveer waited for Asmita, there was someone in the pub who was sipping the same drink that Saveer had ordered. The person's face wasn't visible. The head was titled upwards and a Fedora covered half of the face. A sly smile played on the person's lips. The person, after all, was responsible for bringing Saveer back to his masochistic lifestyle. His pain was the person's pleasure. *It was forever thus*, the person wondered, chewing on the straw in the glass.

Saveer noticed Asmita by the bar, looking around. He immediately received a message from her:

I'm here. Where are you?

Saveer gulped down his LIT. He was tipsy enough to go through it. He stood up and approached Asmita.

'I'm here,' he said. For a moment, she couldn't take her eyes off of him. He was more than what her friends had told her. And immediately her mind said: would he be more than what her friends had told her in bed as well?

'Should we go where we would be in a few hours or would you like to indulge in some small talk at first?'

Asmita knew that the Mean Monster was no-bullshit guy. She cleared her throat and said, 'I want to drink a little.' *Else I wouldn't be able to handle his sex-on-legs vibe*, she thought.

'What are you into?' he asked.

'Teq shots,' she said.

'Teq shots for the lady, please,' Saveer told the bartender. The bartender placed six shots in front of Asmita, who downed them sooner than she usually did.

'Let's go,' she said, taking a deep breath.

Once Saveer and Asmita had left the pub, the person put down the LIT, stood up and went to the women's washroom. Humming a Hindi movie song, the person admired the long hair in the mirror, took out a lipstick and dabbed some of it on the lips. The person was immersed in the reflection in the mirror when someone said, 'Excuse me.' It was a girl.

'Sure, dear,' the person said. The girl frowned. There was something uncanny about the person. But before she could understand what had caught her attention, the person left the washroom.

* * *

It was an awkward drive for Asmita. She talked as much as she could, but Saveer stayed quiet except for occasional monosyllabic utterances. They were heading to her place in Malleswaram. Had he not been so irresistibly sexy and had she not been told so much about him, Asmita would have asked him to stop. She wasn't into random sexual encounters except for one or two instances when she had been drunk. In this case, she only wanted to experience the Mean Monster.

They stopped at her place. The ground floor belonged to the landlord. He followed her upstairs. The moment she unlocked the door, Saveer held her tightly from behind. They stumbled a bit and got inside. Saveer kicked the door close. His lips were all over the nape of her neck as his hands grabbed her thighs. Saveer didn't want to think about anything but he couldn't win over his mind. The way he had made love to Prisha on the yacht flashed in front his eyes. His grasp on her thighs loosened. He took it as a challenge against his own self and thrust his hand under her dress, reaching for her panty. Asmita was already breathing heavily. She felt her panty being tugged down. Saveer was about to probe her vagina when Prisha's body, after it was pulled out of the abyss, floated in front of him. Saveer's hand retreated. Asmita grabbed it and tried to guide it back to her vagina.

'Touch me,' she said in a rasping voice. Saveer put all his energy into concentrating on the here and now but Asmita could feel the initial passion ebbing. His hands left her. She pulled up her panty and turned around.

'Anything wrong?' she asked.

'I'm sorry. It's just that . . . there is this girl . . .' he stopped. Asmita kept looking at him as he sat down with a thud on a nearby chair.

'Don't tell me you stopped because you love a girl?' Asmita said.

'I'm sorry,' Saveer mumbled.

And I thought all men are dogs, Asmita murmured softly and went inside, adjusting her dress.

Saveer was blank for a moment. Then he heard his phone beep. It was a message. He took it out from his pocket and checked. It was Prisha. He felt a lump in his throat. The message read: *Why?*

Saveer kept staring at the question till the phone's screen light went out. He wished he had a one-word answer to the message. Or any answer for that matter.

'Here, have some water.' Asmita was back. She held out a bottle to him. 'It will help,' she added.

It won't, Saveer thought.

4

Saveer had not wanted to come across as rude so he had allowed Gauri and Diggy to continue working as interns at G-Punch. But he had made up his mind to ask them to leave once Prisha joined. Along with her. What he hadn't expected was Prisha to drop in at the office two days after she was released from the hospital.

Saveer had walked out of Asmita's place after he had received another message from Prisha. He had drafted many replies like: *I can explain . . . Let's meet and talk . . . Let me call you . . . I'm not responsible for any of this . . . Sorry, I hid things from you . . . I am the only one responsible . . . Prisha, stay away from me . . .* but couldn't send any of them. In the end, Saveer decided to not respond. She would at the most message again. Or perhaps call. But he wouldn't reply. He could accept becoming someone wicked in her eyes but he wasn't ready to take a risk that could lead to someone's death. More importantly, he couldn't pretend that in Prisha lay his happiness, even though it was true. For over time the tattoo had stopped reading like a statement or a claim and started sounding more like a direct threat. There was someone out there who had been doing bad things to him . . . and to his loved ones, for years now. The tattoo was a confirmation. Whether it was only Prisha's fall or if all the deaths had been connected was something he was not sure of yet.

Saveer was in his cabin responding to some official emails when he casually glanced at the small monitor broadcasting the footage from different CCTVs on the office premises. And in one of them he saw Prisha talking animatedly to Krishna. She was holding a piece of paper. Saveer thought it could be the termination letter that he had asked Krishna to give her if at all she ever came back to office. He noticed that Prisha pushed back Krishna slightly and started heading towards his cabin. Before he could take his eyes off the monitor, Prisha had entered the room. Saveer took his time lifting his eyes off the monitor. He looked up to find her looking at him . . . after six long months.

But for her, it had seemed like years. From the time she fell down to the time she laid her eyes on him, it couldn't have been a mere six months, Prisha thought. Though she had many questions but the moment he looked at her, she felt herself burning as if his one look had set her on fire. The kind of fire that can make even the soul dance to the tune of its heat.

Both were waiting for the other to initiate a conversation. Krishna stepped in excusing himself.

Saveer raised his hand and gestured him to leave. Krishna left, closing the door behind him.

'You want me to stop working for G-Punch?' Prisha asked. There was pain in her voice.

'I do.'

'What else do you want from me, Saveer? Just tell me and I will do it for you,' Prisha said.

'Do you want to sit down?' he asked. Prisha plonked down on one of the chairs right opposite Saveer. He pushed a small bottle of Bisleri towards her but she pushed it back towards him. Their eyes were fixed on each other the whole time.

Saveer stood up and locked the cabin door. Prisha's eyes followed him around. The click of the lock made her lick her lips nervously. He sighed deeply, trying to frame the words he should have told her when he had fallen for her.

'I'd asked you to stay away from me, Prisha, hadn't I?'

'I never thought of you as a disease, Saveer. I don't think I ever will. My coming here today is the second proof of it. My message to you the other night, which you didn't care to respond, was the first. If there is something due to which you're asking me to stay away from you then I would appreciate it if you told me about it frankly. If one's partner is honest, it can immunize one against a lot of things,' Prisha said.

Saveer wanted to smile for he had always known that inside the teenager that Prisha was, was a bud of a woman waiting to flower. He was in love with that bud and looked expectantly towards the grand vista of womanhood it promised once it had flowered. But he didn't smile. He got up and sat on the couch on the other side of the room. Staring at the floor, he said, 'There have been deaths in my family. My brother, my parents, my dog, my first crush, my best friend and Ishanvi . . . all of them had died on my birthday. And then it was on my birthday again that you fell off the cliff. So I thought . . .' his voice trailed off.

Prisha pushed back her chair and stood up and walked towards him. Saveer started praying for her to not touch him. Because it wouldn't just be a touch. It would be a war cry for the myriad emotions he had been holding off since she was put inside the ambulance on his birthday. And then they would simply gush out.

'I know you didn't push me off that cliff,' Prisha said. She placed her hand on his shoulder. Saveer closed his eyes and then opened them again. Before she knew it, he had scooped her up in his arms and was kissing her. At that moment, Prisha realized how much she had been waiting for this. The action was only an expression of the passion she had always felt for him. And he for her. Their tongues began a fierce exploration as he placed his hands around her bum while she wound hers around his neck. Every touch brought back memories. And Saveer and Prisha reached out for them, hungrily.

With Prisha clinging to him, Saveer headed towards the window in the cabin. With one hand, he untied the knot and pulled down the blinds. Then he put her down.

Prisha was wearing a floral dress, which Saveer took off. Then it was her bra. Seconds later, it was Saveer's shirt. He broke the smooch and knelt down, rubbing his face against her navel while tugging her panty down to her ankle. She kept pulling his hair as his tongue dipped into her belly button. As he kissed his way up, Prisha went down, unbuckling his belt, unzipping his trousers, pulling it down urgently along with his underwear. She held his erect penis in her hand and slowly jerked it as she stood up again. Saveer pushed his tongue inside her mouth, placed his hand on her bare butts and picked her up. Sex, more often than not, is associated with lust but in that moment both Prisha and Saveer realized that it could also be the result of a deep-seated love for each other. Love, which can be caged but not controlled. Love, which can only be asked to behave but never tamed. Love, which was impossible and thus innately desirable.

Saveer entered Prisha with one thrust. She instantly grabbed the blinds's rope for both support and for the onslaught she knew was coming up. With every new thrust, she kept, quite unintentionally, pulling the rope which made the blinds go up, inch by inch. Light seeped inside the room slowly as Saveer continued thrusting, till the whole cabin was flooded with sunlight.

Saveer turned around. Prisha let go of the rope. The blinds clattered down. While smooching Prisha, he pushed her gently towards his table. He turned her around and while she held on to the table for support, entered her from behind. Saveer nibbled on the nape of her neck and her shoulder. His thrusts were rocking not just Prisha's body but her core as well. She gripped a nearby chair for support.

She had come to the office to ask him what she had in her message the previous night. While lying on the hospital bed for months, she had an inkling that her inner shores were craving the waves which only he could bring forth. However, when he had kissed her minutes ago, she had realized that she didn't just want those waves to crash on her shores but wanted them to flood her, inundate her. Conquer her such that there were no shores left.

Saveer bit her neck hard as he pulled out at the last moment. She turned and kissed him. They were breathing each other's air. It was scribbled all over their faces: they *weren't* done.

Prisha turned and pushed him, rather forcefully, on the couch. Saveer was still hard when he slumped down on the couch with a thud. Prisha straddled him, allowing him to grow stiffer inside her. This time, while she rode him, their eyes remained locked. As if nothing existed beyond them. As if the whole world was a facade. And in the garb of two bodies, only their souls existed.

Prisha came soon and collapsed on his chest, holding him tight. *Come what may*, she thought, *I won't let this love go to waste*. They lay on the couch for half an hour without uttering a single word. Then suddenly, Saveer spoke up.

'I want to show you something,' he said and stood up. He turned around to show Prisha the tattoo. She frowned.

'*I will fuck your every happiness*,' she read softly. And immediately recollected having seen the 'I' tattooed on his back a long time ago. I for Ishanvi, was what Prisha had concluded back then.

'When did you get it inked?' she asked, running her fingers over each word.

'I didn't. I found this tattoo on my back the morning we were supposed to meet at Nandi Hills.'

'That's strange. How could you have not known about it? I have seen it before.'

'You *have* seen the tattoo?'

'Not the entire line. Just the letter 'I'. I thought it stood for Ishanvi.'

Saveer's mouth hung open. He had never inked it himself, ever.

'I have no idea. I have been thinking about it for the last six months. But nothing is making any sense except . . .'

'Except?'

'I have a request. And promise me that you will listen to me,' Saveer said, trying hard not to look crestfallen.

'What is it?'

'We won't meet again. Ever!'

Prisha could have cried then and there. She held back her tears and said, 'Will you be able to live without me?'

'No, I won't be able to,' he grabbed her hand. His touch was warm. 'But I can't risk you getting killed. Don't you still get it, Prisha? There is someone out there who wants to kill you because we got closer. I don't know what his problem is. But my problem is simple: I can't lose you.'

Prisha looked at him for some time. There was a concoction of patience and restlessness in his eyes.

'Don't *you* get it, Saveer? Whoever that person is, doesn't know that I love you more than he can ever hate you,' she said and kissed him hard.

Neither of them knew that that person was sitting in a small cafe right opposite G-Punch and had heard every bit of their conversation and all that they had been up to in that room. Every cufflink of Saveer's was fitted with a microphone. The ones he was wearing was no different. The person finished a cup of cappuccino and thought, *people never understand. That's the whole problem.* The person took a deep breath and murmured, 'Unless, of course, they are made to understand.'

5

Prisha knew she had lost a considerable amount of academic time. It only meant that either she would have to drop a semester or work harder and sit for both the semester exams together. But for that she and her father would have to meet the dean and explain the situation under which she had missed her classes for the last six months.

Saveer wanted to drop her back home but she insisted on going back alone. So Saveer asked Krishna to accompany her to her apartment. Prisha was happy that her gut feeling had been right. With Utkarsh, she had been grossly wrong. With Saveer, the opposite had happened. She wanted to tell him about a lot of things that could possibly be clues to why she was pushed, and why so many people had died on his birthday. Their conversation in the office was interrupted by Krishna as there were a few meetings lined up for Saveer. Prisha had to leave. Not before tearing up the termination letter and telling Saveer that she would be joining back once she had clarity on the academic front.

Although her parents were staying at Zinnia's, Prisha wanted to spend some time with her friends before going back home. The moment she stepped inside the flat, Gauri said, 'Diggy and I have had a bet of Rs 500.'

'What kind of bet?' Prisha asked.

'She thinks Saveer and you must have kissed today and I think not. I mean you guys just met after a long time,' Diggy answered.

'There is a reason why you are forever single,' Gauri taunted him.

'What do you mean? Prisha isn't as *tharki* as you are.'

'We didn't kiss,' Prisha said. Diggy jumped up in joy and started demanding his prize from Gauri. The latter threw an I-am-disappointed look at Prisha.

'I mean we didn't just kiss. We made out like two animals in heat.'

Diggy paused. His mouth hung open. A slow smile spread on Gauri's face.

'You make me proud, bro,' Gauri hugged Prisha and told Diggy, 'You know what to do now.'

Diggy made a face and said, 'You guys were meeting after six months! Who does that kind of thing?'

'People in love!' Gauri said, 'I want the details.'

Prisha was about to begin when her phone rang. It was her mother. She had called her up a couple of times when she was at G-Punch but she hadn't picked up. She knew that Gauri would get a call next. Prisha had messaged Gauri to tell her mother that she was sleeping.

'I think you better take this one. Aunty had called up twice,' Gauri said. Prisha nodded and took the call. She told her that she would be at Zinnia's flat in some time.

'Let's go to Zin's place. I'll tell you what happened in the cab,' Prisha said.

'Cool.' Gauri stood up to get ready.

'Even I want to know,' Diggy whined.

'No! We don't want to spoil you, Mr Saint. Moreover, you'll stay here and finish our assignments. It's your turn, remember?' Gauri sounded as if she was making a declaration. Diggy's face fell.

On their way to Zinnia's, Prisha shared every detail with Gauri.

'Are you serious? You kept pulling the blinds up?' Prisha blushed.

'I wish I had a man in my life right now. I would have sucked him dry. That's how horny I'm.'

The cabbie stared at them. Prisha gestured Gauri to shut up.

'I'm happy, Gauri. I never thought reconnecting with Saveer would be this easy when I was in the hospital. Believe me,' she said with moist eyes. Gauri held her hand and said, 'I'm really happy for you, bro.'

'I know I won't ever meet anyone like Saveer who would love me because of love alone. There's nothing more than that.'

Gauri understood what she meant. Love, often, is a result of many conditional agendas. People mistake love to be a cause when many a time it is only an effect of someone's physical needs. She had experienced it with Sanjeev. He always said that he loved her but his love was limited. Limited to the body. And just like the body, anything that is limited, is destined to die. Every step taken is towards an ending. While a love beyond the body, is a path towards new beginnings.

Prisha and Gauri reached Zinnia's place to find her parents packing.

'Mumma, I thought you are going to stay for one more week,' Prisha said, sitting down on the bed.

'Your sister has school. We'll have to leave. Our tickets are done.'

Ayushee came and hugged Prisha from behind. 'It's been ages since you've come home, Didi. It's waiting for you.'

Prisha frowned. She broke the hug and glared at her mother.

'What's she talking about?'

'We are *all* leaving for Delhi tomorrow.' It was her father.

'What? Why?'

'Why? Don't you know why?' her father said. 'You'll study in Delhi from now onwards.' It was more of an announcement.

Prisha looked at her father, then her mother and at last at Gauri.

'I'm sorry but I can't leave Bengaluru!'

Except for Gauri everyone else looked incredulously at her.

'I mean I can't leave my studies in between,' Prisha clarified.

'Who is asking you to leave your studies?' her father countered. 'You'll get into some Delhi University college. I've had a talk with a friend who has connections.'

'New college, new people . . . I'm comfortable here, Papa. Please, understand.'

With every argument she had with her father, Prisha felt as if she were being taken away from Saveer. If she agreed to her parents' plan then it would be a slow death to her and Saveer's story. He won't be able to come down to Faridabad all the time. And she wouldn't be allowed to leave Faridabad for the next three years. Everything sounded disgusting to her.

'I've had a talk with my head of the department. He said I won't be losing any time,' Prisha sounded desperate.

Gauri gave her a when-did-this-happen look.

'But if I change colleges now, I will lose time. And my friends will get ahead of me,' Prisha said, sitting on the bed. Her father gave her a look. The doctor had asked him to keep Prisha away from stress since the trauma of the accident was yet to sink in. He went to her, caressed her head and said, 'All right. Stay here.'

Prisha jumped up and hugged her father.

'But I want to meet the head of your department before I leave.'

Prisha gulped nervously and glanced at Gauri. The latter had no answer. She looked at her father.

'I hope that shouldn't be a problem,' he said.

'Not at all,' Prisha said.

6

'Are you mad?' Saveer said after listening to Prisha's plan over the phone.

The plan was simple. Her parents had not met the head of her department before. Nor had they met Saveer. Not even in the hospital. Saveer had intentionally not met Mr and Mrs Srivastav. He didn't know what to introduce himself as. *Friend? Boyfriend?* The thirty-five-year-old boyfriend of a twenty-year-old girl? Which father would accept such a relationship? Especially when his daughter was in the Intensive Care Unit. Saveer preferred to stay quiet. And now when Prisha asked him to pose as her professor and talk to her father, he was getting cold feet.

'Listen, Saveer, either you meet him or I'll have to move back to Faridabad,' Prisha said, with a note of finality. After trying to convince him for the past one hour, she realized that shifting to Faridabad was her last shot.

'But where will I meet him?'

'My family has a flight to Delhi in the afternoon. I will convince Papa to meet you before that. In some cafe.'

'In some cafe? Which parent will meet a college professor in a cafe?' Saveer asked, amazed.

'Let me handle that. You just stick to the script please.'

'Script? Is this a film?'

Prisha laughed. 'But you got to agree this is filmy.'

'I swear it is!'

Next day, Saveer reached the Starbucks outlet close to Prisha's college well before time. He carried a few books with him to make it look real—props to the real-life skit that they were going to pull off. He ordered himself a frappe. Prisha and her father arrived ten minutes later.

'I'm so sorry, Rathod sir,' Mr Srivastav said, shaking his hand eagerly as he sat down opposite Saveer.

'I had to disturb you on your holiday,' he added.

Saveer wasn't surprised. Prisha had called him late at night to inform him about the story that she had cooked up with Gauri and Diggy. Saveer was on a holiday with his family and thus on leave. It was after Prisha had specially requested him that he had agreed to meet her father. That's the reason he had chosen the cafe for the meeting and not the college premises.

'And who is going to talk to your real professor to let you sit for both your semester exams together?' Saveer had asked her.

'My local guardian,' Prisha had said, sounding confident and amused.

'Who?'

'My boyfriend, Saveer Rathod, who will act as my local guardian. There are perks of being in a relationship with an older guy, you know.'

'Yeah, right!' Saveer had said. Surely, teenagers nowadays were far more creative and daring than they used to be when he was young.

'It's all right. Prisha is a bright student. So, it's ok,' Saveer told her father.

'She must have told you about the trauma she went through in the last six months.' By the time he finished talking, Prisha's father was overwhelmed. She grasped his hand.

'I know. Prisha told me,' Saveer said as the scene from Nandi Hills flashed in front of his eyes.

'I just want to make sure that she is all right. Not that I doubt my daughter. But . . .'

This time, Saveer leaned towards Mr Srivastav and said, 'I understand. Don't worry. She won't lose any academic time.' Saveer paused and then added, 'And also . . . I'll take care of her.'

For a moment, Saveer and Prisha's eyes locked together. This wasn't part of the script. But it was truer than any other word in the script. *I'll take care of her*, it reverberated within her.

'Thank you, so much. Students need more mentors like you,' Mr Srivastav said, feeling confident about Prisha's decision.

The meeting lasted for five more minutes after which Prisha and her father took Saveer's leave. Prisha texted Saveer that she would meet him at the office after dropping off her parents at the airport. Saveer told her that he would send Krishna to fetch her.

* * *

The moment Prisha entered Saveer's cabin, she hugged him tight.

'What happened?'

'Don't make me feel so desirable. Okay?'

'Okay,' Saveer smiled.

'Not okay. You don't have to listen to everything I say.'

'O-kay!'

Prisha broke the embrace and looked at him.

'I mean not okay.'

They laughed together. Prisha went and sat down on the couch. Saveer put his laptop on sleep mode.

'I have thought hard,' she said, looking outside through the blinds.

'About?' Saveer pulled up a chair and sat next to her.

'The voice was similar to yours.'

'Whose voice?' Saveer frowned.

'Let me tell you from the beginning. The first time I had a feeling that you were hiding something from me was when I spotted you in the mall while you told me that you were driving to the mall.'

'When was this?'

'Remember the flash mob we did for G-Punch?'

Saveer nodded.

'When the flash mob ended, I saw you. On the first floor.'

'You saw me?' Saveer looked genuinely taken aback. Prisha nodded and said, 'I chased that person but lost him in the crowd.'

'You sure you saw *me*?'

Prisha seemed thoughtful. It was clear that she was trying to recall that day.

'Almost you. I mean, I don't know. He was wearing aviators. Had a similar jawline like yours and . . . the voice was similar to yours as well. Slightly heavier.'

'You talked to him?'

'Before I was pushed off the edge, the person told me that he was sorry. That forever was a lie. I turned around but someone flashed a light in my face so I couldn't see anyone. But . . .'

'But?'

'He visited me in the hospital.'

'He did? When?!'

'One night. I don't remember the date. But not recently. Basically what he said was that he had been killing people for many years now.' *And that he would kill me if we got any closer*, she didn't tell him the last bit lest he panicked.

'This means that all those deaths were never a coincidence?' It sounded more like a question that he was asking himself.

'That goes back twenty-five years!' Saveer mumbled, amazed.

'There's something even more disturbing,' Prisha said, feeling her throat go dry as she thought about what she was going to tell him next.

'What is it?'

'The night he visited me in the hospital, I saw him leaving. And he was in a woman's attire.'

'A woman's attire?' Saveer's had a deep frown on his face. 'The obvious reason could be to hide his real identity.'

'Yeah, I thought so too.'

Saveer stood up and started pacing in the room.

'The tattoo . . .' Prisha said. Saveer shot an inquiring glance at her.

'I had seen the first letter 'I' but I thought you always had it. I for Ishanvi, you see.'

'When did you see it?'

'Again, I don't remember the date but we were on the terrace and . . .' Prisha realized that Saveer wasn't really interested in the conversation. He looked distressed. She stood up and walked towards him. Then she cupped his face in her hands and said, 'Don't get stressed out.'

'There are just too many inexplicable things happening.'

'I know. I have thought about them as well but nothing made sense. But don't get stressed out.' She kissed the tip of his chin.

'I don't know who is behind all this. Why is he doing what he is doing? All I know is that I can't lose you.'

'And I can't lose us.'

Saveer pursed her mouth shut with his own and they stayed like that for a while. Once the kiss broke, Prisha asked, 'Tell me something, did you ever have any enemy or did you ever do something to someone who may be holding a grudge against you or . . .?'

'This has been happening for the last twenty-five years, Prisha! I was just a ten-year-old when it first happened. How much damage can a ten-year-old do to anyone? In fact, what can a ten-year-old do really?'

Nobody said anything after that. But the person sitting in the cafe opposite G-Punch kept toying with a coffee mug and repeating Saveer's last words: *what can a ten-year-old kid do really?*

'A ten-year-old kid can be a murderer,' the person said aloud to nobody in particular and smirked.

7

The last six months had been a testing period for Zinnia. No alcohol, no sex and no outing. The reason: Prisha's parents were staying with her. Although her father and her sister visited only during the weekends, her mother had been staying with her for the past six months. And Zinnia's mother was Prisha's mother's kitty-party friend. Zinnia knew for a fact that if she stuck to her normal lifestyle, it would be reported to her mother and before she knew it, even her parents would come over and start living with her. She practised an unwilling abstinence. There were one or two instances when she went out citing group studies with friends but such occasions were rare. And now when Prisha was out of the hospital and her parents had flown back, it was time for her to go back to living her life her way.

She wanted to go out with her friends first but then decided to go for a Tinder date instead. She started hounding for profiles. She swiped two profiles right, matched with one and was about to give up, when she came across a profile. The name read: The Mean Monster.

Zinnia frowned. *How could it be?* Saveer still sleeps around? As far as she had guessed, Prisha was in a relationship with him. It was quite obvious when she had bumped into her that night in a resto-bar. Zinnia swiped right after staring at the profile thoughtfully. To her surprise, it said there was a match. It meant that the Mean Monster had already liked her profile. Zinnia messaged: *hi! Nice to see you again.*

After some time, a response came: *I was waiting for you.*

Zinnia felt funny between her legs after reading the message. She would never forget the night Saveer had sexually edged her. She could have killed him for delaying her orgasms but then she enjoyed it way more than she thought she would have.

Can we meet tonight? Zinnia messaged.

Of course.

These words switched on her crave-button.

Where? she asked.

My place.

The fact that Saveer didn't want to waste time, that he had invited her over to his place, which was highly unusual for the Mean Monster made Zinnia feel special. Was Saveer interested in her?

Sure. What time?

11.30 p.m. Be on time.

You can count on me.

The next message contained Saveer's address.

* * *

This was the first time Zinnia had come to Saveer's house. She glanced at her watch as she rang the doorbell. It was exactly 11.30 p.m. A message popped up on her Tinder.

Hi, the door is open. Step in. And then come up. Zinnia had a naughty smile on her face. She understood that it must be some sort of a game.

Okay. Zinnia replied and pushed open the door. As she entered, the living room lit up. She looked around and found a staircase. The house was eerily quiet. Zinnia took a deep breath and started climbing up the stairs. However, she slowed down after seeing Saveer's photographs with Prisha and a few others with another girl. She focused on the ones with Prisha. *Was he done with her?* she thought while climbing up.

She entered the bedroom. Except for a dim light next to the door, the room was dark.

'Saveer?'

'I like the way my name sounds when you say it.'

Zinnia smiled. So he was there, she thought. His voice sounded slightly heavier than usual. The game—or whatever it was—was on.

'What's up?' she said. Her voice quivered a little.

'Come on in.'

'Don't tell me the Mean Monster has become kinkier since the last time I had him,' Zinnia said, stepping further inside the room. The light above the bed switched on. She still couldn't see him.

'Where are you?'

'Right here.'

Zinnia turned around to see the silhouette of a man sitting on a chair in the corner.

'What do you see on the bed?' the person asked.

A few things were scattered on the bed. With an amused smile, she said, 'I see a blindfold, a handcuff, a feather and a butt-plug.'

'State your preference for the night.'

Zinnia swallowed nervously. Was it going to be this kinky? she thought, feeling slightly wet. She had never used sex toys ever. And she wasn't sure if she should. She opted for the safest option available.

'Blindfold,' she said.

'Wear it.'

'What do you have in mind, Monster?' Zinnia asked. She had started enjoying the game. When she had found out that Prisha had befriended Saveer, she was jealous. But she had never taken that jealousy seriously until she saw him on Tinder hours ago. Prisha had busted a myth for her. Zinnia was told that the Mean Monster never involved himself with anyone. But he did with Prisha. And tonight he was about to break another rule. She knew he never repeated his girls. But tonight he would.

Suddenly, she saw the possibility of stretching one night with the Monster into a full-fledged date. Even the thought of flaunting the Mean Monster as her boyfriend gave Zinnia a mental orgasm.

'I only can only picture you naked now.'

Zinnia wasted no time in wearing the blindfold. She was told to strip next. She did. Zinnia had never been this acutely conscious of being naked before.

'I'm waiting for you,' she said. Seconds later, she felt his hands on her thighs. His touch seemed softer than before. She felt his lips on her outer thighs first and then on her inner thighs. Her wet vaginal lips were expecting his tongue but instead she felt the tip of a hard dick. Intertwining his fingers with Zinnia's, the person pinned her hands above her head. She lifted up her head while moaning loudly. The dick was unbelievably hard! And as the thrusts began, Zinnia felt as if she were being transported to some other place. There was no edging this time but he did give her multiple orgasms. And although Zinnia had enjoyed the session despite her doubts, she had failed to guess that she had been fucked by a strap-on dildo and not a real penis. By the time she was allowed to rest, Zinnia had climaxed four times. She felt drained. She lay on the bed for some time before opening the blindfold. She sat up, looking around for the Mean Monster. She found him sitting in the corner, his legs stretched out. They were perfectly waxed, shining nut-brown.

'I loved it, Saveer,' she said.

'I'm glad you did. I've a request though.'

'Sure, what is it?'

'Don't tell any of this to Prisha.'

Zinnia instantly felt victorious. The statement was sheer pleasure to her ears. She was the one who had experienced the Mean Monster before Prisha. How could the latter just take him away from her?

'I never will,' Zinnia said and a moment later, added, 'But do I need to catch you again through Tinder?' Zinnia tried to confirm her gut feeling.

'No. We will meet again. Soon.'

Zinnia smiled to herself.

'I need to use the washroom,' she said.

'On the right.'

'Thanks.'

A naked Zinnia stood up and went towards the washroom. She stopped next to the door and said, 'Can we take a selfie together?'

The response wasn't immediate.

'Get dressed first.'

'Sure. I'll be quick.' Zinnia went inside the washroom and closed the door behind her.

The person stood up and walked towards a small mirror in the room. Using a lipstick, the person wrote something on the mirror. Then applied it on the lips.

'This shade of red suits me,' the person said and smiled at her reflection.

Zinnia came out of the washroom after some time. She called out to Saveer but there wasn't any answer. She picked up her bra from the floor but didn't find her panty. While looking for it, Zinnia's eyes fell on the mirror. There was something written in red:

Let your panty be with me. Lock the main door. Keep the keys by the gate. A cab is waiting for you. Wipe this off after you've read it.

Zinnia had a wicked smile on her face. It was clear that Saveer was done with Prisha. She knew they weren't compatible. Saveer needed someone like her. She rubbed off the message and left.

Before climbing into the cab, she noticed a woman standing under a lamp post. Light from the lamp post lit up only half of the woman's body, her face remained in darkness. The cab sped away.

The woman walked up to the main gate and picked up the keys left behind by Zinnia.

'It feels awesome to fuck you up this way, little one. No more killings. And yet the pain would be . . . perhaps more,' she said softly, to nobody.

8

'I'm having these weird sleeping disorders,' Saveer said as he drove slowly to his office through heavy traffic.

'What happened?' Prisha asked. She had accompanied Gauri and Diggy to Shivam Snacks Corner, a popular eating joint near her college. Gauri and Diggy were hogging their breakfast, onion butter Maggi, while Prisha was on a call with Saveer.

'Remember, I had told you that I had overslept and failed to meet you once when we had to go to Nandi Hills?'

'Yes.' Prisha walked away from the crowd around the snacks corner so she could hear Saveer clearly.

'Also, remember when we had the flash mob, you had said that you had ended up driving in the same area for a while,' Prisha reminded him.

'Right. I had slept off then as well.'

'Did it happen last night as well?'

'Exactly. I remember sitting down for dinner last night but I slept like a log after that. And woke up . . .'

'Woke up . . . where?'

'Under my bed.'

'What? Under your bed?'

'I know it's absurd but it's true.'

'I think you should consult a doctor.'

'I thought so too. I will go this evening.'

'All right. I will meet you in the evening. I have a couple of lectures now,' Prisha said.

'Yep, fine.'

Prisha disconnected the call not understanding one bit how and why someone would sleep under their bed. She walked back to the snacks corner, thoughtful. She stood behind Gauri and Diggy. And that's when she noticed Gauri talking to a guy. She nudged Diggy. 'Who is he?'

'I don't know his name. But I've seen him talking to Gauri a few times in the last two months.'

'You didn't ask her?'

'No. I know he is from our college.'

Prisha and Diggy waited for Gauri to finish talking. Once she was done, she turned around to find her friends looking at her inquiringly.

'What?' she shrugged and started walking towards the college. The other two caught up with her.

'Who is that guy?' Prisha asked. 'Diggy said he has seen you talking to him for the last two months now.'

'He is Karthik. Our junior,' Gauri said.

'And . . . ?' Prisha insisted.

'And he loves me.'

'You are telling me this, now?! I want to know the whole story!'

'There is no story, bro. He saw me at the fresher's months ago. Then he approached me saying that he likes me. I avoided him. He came back saying that he still loves me. So I lied that I'm committed and told him to stay away from me. But he came back again, saying that he had found out that I'm not committed.'

'Why did you lie? If you aren't interested, then just tell him so,' Diggy said.

'I told him today that I'm not interested,' Gauri said, without looking at either of them.

'Hmm, good.'

Prisha had an inkling that she might be lying. But she didn't probe any further.

They went back to attending lectures. During a break, Zinnia approached Prisha while she was on a call with Saveer.

'What's up?' Zinnia asked. Although they had met the day her parents had left for Delhi, she behaved as if they were meeting after a long time. Gauri and Diggy kept walking. They had somehow never warmed up to Zinnia.

'I'm good. What's up with you, Zin?' Prisha asked.

'All good and glowing. So, did you get to meet Saveer?'

The question was sudden and Prisha couldn't help but stare at her.

'Just asking,' Zinnia clarified.

'Yeah, I did.' *Does she know that Saveer and I are together? But how would she? I never told her. And Saveer . . . he wouldn't meet her*, Prisha thought.

'Nice. Hope he is good.'

'He is.' Prisha was slightly curt this time.

'You take care. Catch you soon,' Zinnia said. There was a hint of amusement on her face which Prisha couldn't decode but she had a hunch that something was not quite right.

She joined the other two.

'What was the BC saying?' Gauri asked.

'Nothing,' Prisha said.

'Anyway, I need to go to the mall,' Gauri said.

'Cool. Let's go. I'll meet Saveer after that,' Prisha said.

'Not cool,' Diggy said. 'I'm feeling sleepy. I was working on my assignment all night long. I guess, I'll go home and crash.'

Diggy took his leave while the girls went to Forum Mall. It was after they had entered the mall that Gauri told Prisha, 'I lied.'

'About?'

'Karthik. I didn't tell him that I am not interested.'

'Which means you are?'

'Yes. In destroying him.'

Prisha frowned. She dragged Gauri to the first floor and standing next to a vacant corner, asked, 'What are you saying? Just tell me everything clearly.'

'I like him,' Gauri said, 'but I don't want him to get me easily. Everyone has that one love which they crave for but never attain. I want to be that love for Karthik. I will invite him but I won't be there to welcome him.'

Prisha didn't know how exactly to react.

'Why are you so complicated, Gauri? Why would you do this to anyone?' Prisha sounded a little helpless.

'Why should I be the only one who lost? Let him also understand that just because he says he likes or loves me, I won't be his. Just like . . .' Her voice trailed off. Prisha understood who Gauri had in mind. They roamed around the mall quietly. Prisha went out after she got a call from Saveer. He wanted to meet at a cafe but she insisted on visiting him at home.

* * *

'Whoever is playing games with you and me, needs to know we don't give a fuck. Otherwise, he will never come out,' Prisha said, hugging Saveer tightly. He nodded.

'That's the best way to force him to commit a mistake which would lead us to him. Else, right now even involving the police seems pointless,' Saveer said.

'Just what I meant.' She kissed him on his lips.

'I like that I have to stand on my toes to get to your lips.' She kissed him again.

'And . . .' Saveer placed his hands on her butt and picked her up, saying, 'I like to feel your soft bum when you kiss me.' They smooched for some time before collapsing on the couch together.

'Do you think everyone has that one someone whom they crave for but never get?' Prisha asked. Saveer was lying on the couch while she was lying on top of him. Her head was on his chest. She had unbuttoned his shirt till his torso. She could smell him as she talked. His right hand was on her head and the left one was on her back.

'I think so,' Saveer said. Prisha immediately knew who he had in mind.

'I crave for you, Saveer,' Prisha said, lifting her head up and looking into his eyes. 'And I don't think I'll ever crave like this for anyone again. But I don't want you to be the one I never get.' She planted a dry kiss on his lips.

'I don't want to lose you either,' he said, kissing her back. For some time, their faces were so close that they were inhaling each other's breaths. She simply rubbed her face against his.

'You know,' she whispered. 'Utkarsh and my relationship had no fear. I was too happy. Too secure. Too comfortable. But after meeting you, I realized how wrong that was. Every genuine, intense relationship has something to fear. Just like pain makes one feel alive, fear makes a relationship real. Even when I was in the hospital, I wanted to survive so I could be close to you. For forever. I had this fear: what if by the time I was released, things changed between us? What if we didn't pick up where we had left? But my ultimate fear is what if we don't go the distance? Means, doesn't matter. But what if . . .'

Saveer held her face and said, 'When you were in the hospital, I had given up on our love story. I had sworn I would not come near you. I had even activated the Mean Monster avatar.'

'What?'

'That's true.'

'You mean you fucked girls when I was in the hospital?'

'No. I activated the number after you were discharged. But it was a disaster. I simply couldn't do it.'

'Good for you,' Prisha said, sounding strict. A smile spread over Saveer's face as he continued.

'But now you have changed my views. I have realized that every relationship also needs an assurance along with fear. Fear and assurance are the yin and the yang in a relationship. My ultimate assurance is that I am yours, come what may. Nothing else matters. I will always be yours.' He planted a kiss on her forehead.

They lay silent for some time.

'Did you meet Zinnia ever?' Prisha asked. It was an impulsive question, she knew. And she didn't know why she had to ask it.

'Zinnia?'

'The girl you . . .'

'No, I didn't. Why?'

'Nothing. By the way, did you talk to a doctor?'

'I have an appointment this week,' Saveer said and after a thoughtful pause, added, 'Who sleeps under a bed!'

'Let me know whenever you meet the doctor,' Prisha said with motherly concern. She held him tightly and closed her eyes, making herself comfortable on his chest.

* * *

Diggy was irritated as he got out of the department store. Gauri had not only woken him up but also kicked his ass repeatedly till he agreed to go out and get her Maggi noodles. The stock in the house had depleted. He wasn't her boyfriend that he would take care of her tantrums all the time. He was muttering to himself as he entered the lane to his apartment. He saw a car parked opposite the main gate. Then he saw a woman getting inside the car. Whether she was coming back from the small cigarette shop down the lane or the apartment ahead he couldn't tell. But as she was about to lock the door, Diggy noticed something fall on the ground. She had not seen it. He raised his voice and walked briskly and retrieved a phone that had fallen on the road. He knocked on the car's window. The woman rolled it down.

'Excuse me, this fell down,' he said. The woman took the phone.

'How nice of you!' she said.

'It's all right,' Diggy smiled.

'What's your name?'

'Digambar Sethia.'

'Thank you, Digambar.' the woman said, rolling up the window. The next second, she drove past Diggy. *She is easily the most beautiful woman I've ever seen*, Diggy thought.

9

Prisha couldn't tell if her phone was actually ringing or if she was dreaming. She opened her eyes slightly and saw her phone flashing Saveer's name. Her heart skipped a beat. She sat up and took the call.

'Hey, what's up?' she said groggily.

'How long does it take for you to get ready?'

'What?' she glanced at the time on her phone: 8 p.m.

'How long does it take for you to get ready?' Saveer repeated.

'Umm . . . mmm . . . five minutes? But why?' The moment she finished, Prisha heard someone honk loudly outside her apartment.

'Did you hear that?'

'Fuck you!' she yelled and scampered off to the window.

Saveer had told her that he had a meeting with a client in the evening, which might run late into the night. Prisha had skipped office to attend her lectures. She had come home and gone off to sleep after setting an alarm for midnight. She wanted to wish him at the stroke of the midnight hour. Prisha had seen him for the first time at Zinnia's place on that day. And so much had happened since then.

As Prisha looked down from the window, she spotted Saveer on his bike. He was carrying a rucksack and a saddlebag was secured to the back of his motorcycle.

'Your time starts now,' he said over the phone; he was grinning at her. Prisha washed her face, stuffed a few clothes into a small duffle bag, wore a cropped top, pulled on a pair of shorts and her sneakers, and dashed out.

'What's happening?' she said, boarding the pillion seat.

'We shall celebrate this special day in a special way,' he said. Prisha put her arms around him and they roared into the night.

They chatted for a while but mostly remained quiet during the course of the journey. She didn't even ask him where they were heading. She only wished for the path to never end. *How amazing would it be if I got down from the bike to realize that it's afterlife* . . . Prisha wondered.

They stopped twice on the Bengaluru-Coorg highway. Once for refuelling and once to have dinner. Prisha was pleasantly surprised when she realized that Saveer had made the dinner himself.

'Don't you make me fall for you every day, okay?' she said, coming close to him and biting his ears.

'All right.' He looked amused.

'Listen to me always!' she said, grabbing his T-shirt. They looked at each other fiercely. And they knew that they were desiring each other carnally in their minds. Prisha let go of his T-shirt.

'Now tell me where we are going?' she intentionally changed the topic.

'You'll see,' he said. Few minutes later, they were on the road again, cruising on the highway. They stayed quiet. When two hearts are in love, silence gives voice to feelings. And Prisha was enjoying being kissed by those feelings, which she had conceived with him, within her.

It was an hour to midnight when they finally reached their destination: Harangi Dam on the way to Coorg. Saveer parked the bike next to a big tree and unloaded their belongings. They traipsed down a pebbly path towards the calm backwater with Prisha lighting the way using her phone's torchlight. Saveer found a supposedly safe spot and placed the bags on the ground. In the next half an hour, while Saveer was busy setting up the tent that he had brought, Prisha couldn't believe that she had been this lucky. That after a life storm, a love rainbow was possible. She had moist eyes but she kept responding to Saveer's questions, not letting him know anything. There are certain things that cannot be shared even with your soulmate. You have to wait for them to understand on their own.

Once Saveer was done lighting the last scented candle inside the tent, Prisha crawled inside it. There was a cosy sleeping bag and love candles on four corners of it. Just like her, they too were burning bright. They talked for a long time, sipping red wine that Saveer had brought in his rucksack. Some time in between, an alarm went off. It was Saveer's phone. He dismissed it.

'It's twelve,' he said.

'You had once told me that forever is a lie,' Prisha said. They were lying inside the bag, facing each other. Their faces were lit up in the glow of the warm candle light. The scene looked right out of a fairy tale. As if it could not be happening as much it was happening.

'And now I'm telling you . . . forever is true.'

Prisha placed her palm on his forehead and ran down her fingers till his chin.

'This forever?' she asked softly.

Saveer nodded. He kissed her hard and then said, 'This forever, where the echo of this kiss shall reach. This is true.'

Only Prisha knew how far the echo of the kiss went. Right into her. Where her soul was, creating ripples in the most beautiful way possible.

'You know, the night Ishanvi had died, I had made a similar tent for her in our Mumbai flat.' Saveer sounded forlorn.

It struck Prisha like a slap. *Was she everything that he couldn't get from Ishanvi?* She immediately dismissed the thought. Saveer never made her feel that way, nonetheless, it was something that always gnawed at her.

Prisha pushed back Saveer gently. She didn't want to discuss Ishanvi. Not now, not ever. She unzipped the cover of the sleeping bag and got on top of him. With an urgency, she took off his T-shirt. He wanted to slide his hands under her top but Prisha pinned them down.

'Not tonight, Monster. You aren't in control. Tonight, I'm the one in control.' She smirked. Saveer folded his hands behind his head and readied himself for the show.

Prisha bent down and kissed his forehead, his cheeks, his nose and then bit his lower lip, hard. It tore slightly and started bleeding a little, which she sucked out clean. With a devilish smile, she kissed her way down to his torso. Then she bit him there. Saveer caught her hand in response.

'You aren't allowed to move your hand, Monster,' she said, giving him the I-will-eat-you-up-alive look, unbuckled his belt, unbuttoned the jeans and tugged them down.

Prisha spread his legs and started caressing his groin.

'Someone's growing,' she said, stifling a giggle.

'With so much love, what else will that someone do?' Saveer said.

Prisha slowly pulled down his underwear. She grabbed his erect penis and started massaging its hard shaft. With her other hand, she drew goosebumps on his turgid balls with her nails. His penis immediately became stiffer.

'Whoa! It seems like someone has recently read up on a few things,' Saveer quipped, enjoying every bit of it. For him, it was a role reversal.

'To catch a monster, set a monster,' Prisha winked. She'd used her free time in college googling 'how to give pleasure to a man'. And now it was time to regurgitate what she had learnt. Moreover, she had always resented that in giving pleasure Saveer was always ahead of her. Tonight, she wanted to catch up with him.

The way she toyed with his penis—sucking, jerking it, points where she pressed hard and rolled her tongue over the shaft—he knew she was trying to edge him. When she licked his perineum, Saveer felt that he would come right then but she didn't let him.

'How does it feel getting a taste of your own medicine?' Prisha asked with a naughty smile. Saveer glared at her and then leapt up and picked her up in his arms.

'Saveer!' she screamed with fear and excitement. He carried her out of the tent in his arms—both butt naked—and headed straight towards the backwater. Prisha told him to put her down but Saveer asked her to be quiet lest someone came up. He walked into the backwater slowly along with Prisha. Her body started shivering in the cold water. She held on to Saveer tightly as he kissed her trembling lips. His embrace provided her warmth from the biting cold of the water. And so much more, she thought.

'Take me, Saveer. Take me now!' she said. The urgency in her voice aroused him. And Saveer wasted no time in holding her tight and walking back towards the bank. With half of his body still in the water, he got on top of her and entered her. She plucked out fistfuls of dew-laden grass as the thrusts increased in intensity. Saveer grabbed her legs and put them on his shoulder so he could penetrate her completely. In the process, she clawed his back as much as possible as he kept thrusting her deeper and harder. Prisha knew that Saveer could climax any moment. When he came, she felt her soul shudder. They lay there for a while, cuddling. Two intertwined bodies, one coalesced soul, but they didn't know that there had been a spectator to their act. And the person had a problem watching everything. The person had had enough of such fake possibilities that love promised to people.

Saveer was the one who woke up first in the morning, naked inside the tent. He looked around. Prisha was lying next to him. Naked under a bedsheet. He started laughing looking at her. His laughter woke her up. Before she could ask him what was wrong, she got startled seeing his face. Prisha didn't know Saveer was laughing at her because there was a black moustache drawn right under her nose. On the other hand, Saveer didn't know that he had lipstick and mascara on his eyes.

10

Saveer drove faster than he normally did. He was quiet since they had washed their faces in the backwater. Neither of them had to ask who had done it and yet neither of them knew exactly who had done it? But how? And when? The last thing they both remembered was lying naked on the bank close to the break of dawn.

Both of them were immersed in their thoughts. Prisha wasn't clinging to Saveer the way she had last night. She sensed a leave-me-alone-for-sometime vibe from Saveer though he didn't say anything out loud.

It was only when he stopped next a small roadside *dhaba* for breakfast that Prisha decided to talk to him.

'What are you thinking?' she asked as they were served steaming idlis and filter coffee.

Saveer looked at her and their eyes met momentarily. The first time that day since they had realized someone had played a prank on them while they were sleeping.

'What did I do to deserve this for the last twenty-five years? And because of me so many people have been affected.' He paused and added, 'Affected is actually a soft word.'

Prisha stayed thoughtful for some time. Then her face suddenly darkened. Saveer looked at her.

'I forgot to tell you something. It is important and I don't know how I didn't mention it earlier.'

'What is it?'

'I don't remember the exact day but this was soon after I had spotted someone like you in the mall.' Prisha paused as if she were trying to frame her words.

'I'm listening.'

'You'd messaged me one night to come over. I did but you didn't show up. You only guided me to your room where you fingered me after blindfolding me. You were ordering me to do things through messages.'

'You mean I was somewhere else and you were in my room?'

'No! You were right there in the room, in spite of which you were messaging me, asking me to do stuff.'

'Stuff like?'

'Strip myself and . . .'

'Don't tell me you did it!'

'I not only did that,' Prisha's mouth had gone dry, 'but was fingered to an orgasm.' She felt a knot in her stomach while confessing it.

Saveer kept staring at his coffee. Prisha didn't know what to say next. A minute later, Saveer said, 'Except for the voice, was there anything else which led you to believe that it was me?'

Prisha frowned. She thought hard but no matter how much she tried, she only had broken memories of that night. She shook her head. There was nothing else that she remembered.

'Oh! But I woke up in my flat. When I asked my landlady, she said that I had been dropped home by a woman.'

'Did the landlady see the woman's face?'

'No.'

'I'm sure this woman thing is an only an alias. There is a man behind it. The fact that he visited you in the hospital dressed as a woman confirms it.'

'Or there are two people involved. A woman and a man,' Prisha thought out loud.

'Could be,' but Saveer didn't sound convinced. He gulped down his coffee and was about to get up when he sat back down with a thud.

'What happened?'

'I remember seeing the silhouette of a woman months ago when I had driven up to Nandi Hills one night,' Saveer said, recalling the night when his bike had fallen on the ground and he had seen the outline of a woman in the glow of his motorcycle's headlight. She was gone in the blink of an eye.

'That was the only time? Are you sure you haven't or hadn't seen her earlier or later?'

'Only time.' The words barely escaped Saveer. 'But there is another dot which, right now, seems to connect the previous dots.'

'What is it?'

'I wonder how you were brought back to your house from mine. And how did we end up inside the tent when we had fallen asleep next to the backwater? More importantly, why did we fall asleep on the bank?'

'What do you mean?'

'I think this guy, whoever he is, has been sedating me. And that night, perhaps you too had been sedated. And last night, I think the same thing happened.'

'But you brought home-cooked food, right?' Prisha said. Saveer gave her a look and she understood. It didn't mean it could not have been spiked. And it further confirmed that the person had access to Saveer's house. For a moment, Prisha felt scared. She wished she could simply vanish from that place with Saveer. Someplace, where there wasn't anybody to upset their love story. The next second, she realized she was being wistful. Their best bet to stop all this was to get to the person.

'I'm sorry I may sound insensitive,' Prisha said, 'but do you mind if I ask you how other people in your family died? Like I know how Ishanvi died. What about your best friend? Or your crush?'

Saveer took a few minutes before he narrated how Aditri had died.

'And what about the others? Someone whose death bothered you a lot?' Prisha asked.

Saveer's mind started racing.

* * *

From Saveer's memory
His uncle and best friend
1991 to 2008

My best friend's name was Piyush. We had been friends since I was twelve. It was the year after my uncle had suffered a cerebral stroke. In fact, I should first tell you about my uncle and then about Piyush.

Raghuveer Rathod, my uncle, had renounced the world at an early age. He was twenty-three when he had announced to my grandparents that he would become a sannyasi and live a detached life in some ashram in the hills. Although everyone, from my grandparents to my parents, objected as he was the youngest in the family but he seemed to be under some spell and was adamant to leave home. Nobody knew who had inspired him or 'brainwashed' him, as my father used to put it, into it. My uncle left and came back when he was thirty. I was around three or four years old back then. The images are pretty blurred in my mind. I remember he took my brother along with him. My parents told me that my brother was going to spend some time with my uncle.

It was during my tenth birthday that I was told that he was no more. Now that I come to think of it, I was so young back then that I don't even have any concrete memories of him. Raghu uncle had taken him a little too early. I felt sad when I got to know about his death but simply because everybody else was. His name was Veer Rathod. I don't know how exactly he died. Nobody ever spoke much about him.

Anyway, on my eleventh birthday, Raghu uncle was supposed to visit us with his disciples from the ashram. He had some work in the city. But news came that he had been bitten by a snake. Owing to the trauma, he suffered a cerebral stroke and since then has been paralysed. He is the only person alive in my family, but then again he isn't really alive in that way, if you know what I mean. I loved my uncle. He used to teach me good things. And I missed him even though he would rarely visit us. I'm not sure how he is now. I haven't heard from him for a long time now.

It was a year later that I met Piyush in school. He was everything I was not back then. He was daring, rebellious, the teachers' pet, good in studies and someone who was an example for other kids. For me, he was like a brother. Someone I could go to with all my problems because even though we were of the same age, he was more mature than me. We did our schooling together. He was a great emotional support when Aditri died. Without him, I don't think I would have ever regained my focus in academic life after her death. Come to think of it, he was the one person who had been with me on every birthday of mine since the deaths started happening. Till, of course, I turned twenty-five. By then, I had lost everyone in my family. Piyush was working in Pune while I was in Mumbai. He had arrived on time for my birthday. We were supposed to catch up as we were meeting after almost a year back then. But since he arrived, Piyush looked disturbed. He looked at me as if I had told him something terrible. I kept asking him if there was something wrong but he didn't say anything. Then he said that he was going to make a call as there was no network in my flat. When he didn't return for over an hour, I got curious. Before I could find him, the security guard of my building rang the doorbell and informed me that Piyush had jumped off from the roof. I rushed downstairs and found him lying on the ground, his head squashed. There was a suicide note as well. It stated that he wasn't satisfied with his career and had thus killed himself. His parents filed a police case refusing to believe that he had committed suicide. I was with them. Piyush wasn't someone who would kill himself. In fact, he had such zest for life that others drew inspiration from him. How could such a man kill himself? When the handwriting on the note was tested, it turned out to be his. And thus, every other theory was put to rest.

I still miss him.

11

There was an uncomfortable silence between the two.

'What about your dog?' Prisha asked.

'*Piano* was with me for five years. On my nineteenth birthday, he simply disappeared. Nowhere to be found. I remember I cried my eyes out that day. But that which is not supposed to come back to you, doesn't really return. Does it? And you have to live with that eventuality,' Saveer sighed.

Prisha felt helpless seeing Saveer resigned. What could he have possibly done to have deserve such a cruel fate? If someone was deliberately doing it, which was the obvious now, then it wasn't even fate. To see your loved ones dying, one after another, is life at its cruellest. And Saveer had seen so many of them. That too on his birthdays. As if someone was trying to tell him that his birth had been a curse. Could that be a clue? Saveer's birthday? Prisha wanted to ask Saveer, but she kept it to herself. She would ask him later when the time was right. She sensed that he was feeling low.

'Enough of the past,' she said and stood up. 'Let's go.'

Saveer kept some money under his cup and they left.

He dropped Prisha off at her apartment and rode back home. She tried to look chirpy in front of Gauri but felt a strange restlessness within. Masking her feelings, she changed and the two went to college. She felt as if there was bad news in the air.

Prisha attended her lectures and diligently made notes, but she couldn't concentrate on anything. The moment her classes got over, she came home and started googling the names Saveer had mentioned. His uncle, his best friend, his crush, but nothing came up. Considering there was a foul play behind every death, how could all of them have been done so neatly? Every death led to a dead end. Like it would have been with Prisha had she died. It too would have been a cul-de-sac because nobody had seen her being pushed off the cliff. A chill ran down her spine. Who was Saveer and she up against?

Her trance was broken by Diggy, who came prancing along happily after bunking college that day.

'What happened to you?' Gauri was lying beside Prisha and scrolling through new arrivals on her favourite shopping app.

'I just met the most amazing woman ever!' he said. Prisha and Gauri looked at each other.

'Woman? I thought you were into men,' Gauri said.

'Shut up. Even I thought I was into men but this woman made me realize . . .'

'Why are you saying woman?' Prisha asked.

'Because she is a woman! A lady. What a lady!'

Gauri guffawed, 'What's wrong with all three of us? First it was me, then it was Prisha and now it's you. We all only fall for older men and women!'

Prisha couldn't help but laugh.

'She talks such deep stuff. Every sentence of hers is so layered. And looks-wise . . . .' Diggy fanned himself, suggesting that the woman was very hot. He was always too animated with his descriptions.

'Where did you meet her?' Prisha asked.

'Tinder, I'm sure,' Gauri rolled her eyes.

'No! There's a world beyond Tinder.'

'I saw her a few days ago right outside our apartment. She had dropped her phone. I picked it up for her. And today again, she had dropped her handkerchief and I picked it up for her. She remembered my name and invited me over to her place for coffee.'

'Ugh, so filmy!' Gauri exclaimed.

'Seriously!' Prisha joined her.

Diggy's phone rang.

'Jealous, huh?' Diggy told the girls and glanced at this phone. 'OMG! She is calling. Hasta la vista, babies,' Diggy said and disappeared into his room.

'No offence, but I'm sure the woman must be a bored housewife or someone having the fun of her life with him,' Prisha said.

'Let him enjoy. Guess it is his first,' Gauri winked. Prisha smiled and went to get her laptop to complete a college assignment. Gauri went back to her shopping app. After completing her assignment, Prisha called up Saveer but he didn't pick up. She messaged him good night and went off to sleep.

At some point in the night, Prisha woke up feeling thirsty. She gulped down some water from the bottle kept beside her and checked the time on her phone: 2.37 a.m. There were no messages from Saveer. But there was a message from Zinnia. A voice note. She would generally call her rather than sending voice notes on WhatsApp. Since Gauri was sleeping next to her, she plugged in her earphones and tapped on the voice note. Her mouth hung open. All she could hear was Zinnia moaning and yelling: *Saveer, fuck me harder . . . Harder! Harder! Harder!*

12

Prisha couldn't sleep for the rest of the night. The voice note kept echoing in her mind. What was going on? Was Saveer really cheating on her? When the mind is weak, it knits elaborate stories from tiny doubts. Whatever she knew of Saveer was only through him. There was no way she could double-check the stuff he told her. And then a disturbing question occurred to her: what if Saveer indeed was a bad person? Could he really be the guy that the person who had visited her in the hospital had warned about? Prisha hated herself for even considering the thought but she couldn't get it out of her system.

The first thing Prisha did in the morning was visit Zinnia. She had to ring the doorbell thrice before Zinnia opened the door. She looked sleepy. But the moment she registered that it was Prisha, she looked slightly guilty.

'Hey, what's up?' Zinnia said. Prisha didn't wait to be invited in. She stormed inside. Zinnia closed the door behind her.

'I won't pretend any more, Zin. Saveer and I are dating. It has been over a year. And it's not casual either. We love each other.'

Zinnia didn't know what to say. Especially after last night when she had had the best sex of her life. And right now, Zinnia was facing the most embarrassing moment of her life: standing in front of the girl whose boyfriend had fucked her better than the best.

'So . . .?' Zinnia mumbled.

'So, please explain this,' Prisha said, and handed over her phone to her. Zinnia played the voice note on WhatsApp. And embarrassed herself further.

'I didn't send it, Prisha!' she claimed incredulously.

'Then who did? That too from your phone!'

It has to be Saveer, Zinnia thought, *but why would he do such a stupid thing?*

'Listen, I would have told you had Saveer not asked me not to tell you.' Zinnia knew that she couldn't hide the truth any more.

'Tell me what? Saveer asked you to not tell me?' Prisha had a bad feeling about it. Though she had asked the question, she didn't want to know the answer. Somehow, she had an inkling of what was coming up next.

'Saveer and I are in a physical relationship. He asked me not to tell you about it,' Zinnia said and didn't know where to look at.

Prisha was quiet.

'How many times did you guys do it?'

'Twice.' Zinnia felt that it was better to tell Prisha the truth.

'Did it happen when I was in the hospital?'

'No. It happened recently.'

'Where did you guys do it? Here?'

'At his place.'

'At his place?' Prisha wasn't ready for this.

Zinnia nodded. Prisha dashed out of the flat before Zinnia could stop her. She called her up but Prisha didn't pick up the phone. She had come over on Diggy's two-wheeler. Once downstairs, Prisha drove the scooty in full speed and to nowhere in particular. She broke a couple of traffic signals but luckily, there weren't any traffic constables to catch her. She finally stopped on a random lane and leaning against the handlebar of the scooty, started sobbing. The one thing she could never tolerate was sharing her man and that's the one thing that had happened to her, again. Her phone rang. It was Saveer. Her impulse was to throw the phone away but she managed to overpower it and took the call.

'Sorry, I overslept. Couldn't take your call last night,' Saveer said. He sounded sleepy.

Of course, men often sleep peacefully after a good fucking session, Prisha thought and asked, 'Where were you last night?' The bluntness in her voice made Saveer realize that something was wrong.

'At my place. Where else?'

'Okay.'

'Let's meet in an hour?'

'No.'

'What happened?'

'Nothing. I'll talk to you later,' she had to try hard to stop her voice from breaking in front of him. She switched off her phone and started crying again, not knowing what to believe in. Trust is a weird thing. You know you can't ever be sure of it and yet you have to be sure of it. It is this choice that feels like a constraint. She trusted Saveer else she would never have come this far knowing his past. She also knew that there was someone trying to sabotage Saveer's relationships. And yet a doubt had seeped in, which was enough to rage a war inside her.

Prisha was unusually quiet in college. Gauri nudged her but she didn't say anything. Not until Diggy went to meet his new friend.

'There's a problem,' Prisha said. They were in a CCD outlet close to their apartment.

'I knew it. Come on, tell me, bro,' Gauri said, pushing away her cafe latte and focusing her attention on Prisha. The latter took a few minutes to tell her everything.

'I always knew Zinnia was a bitch,' Gauri said.

'She might be one but whatever she told me was true.'

'Why did she fuck Saveer anyway? She knew he was yours, right?' Gauri was furious.

'Not really. I never mentioned it.'

Gauri thought for a few seconds and then said, 'Just talk to Saveer. Judge his reaction. And then ask him for an explanation. He owes you one!'

'I know. It's just that . . .' Prisha took some time before saying, 'I'm scared. Too scared to lose him. Doesn't matter what the reason might be. But I can't lose him.'

'I totally get it. I know how the fear of losing the one who is your world feels like. I also know what happens when you are told that the world that you thought was yours isn't any more. That you have to find another world and call it yours until, of course, it too runs the danger of being snatched away from you because no matter how much our love-struck hearts convince us, nobody can be ours forever.' It was more of a release of Gauri's pent-up emotions than her assessment of Prisha's predicament.

'But before everything, are you sure Zinnia went to his house?' Gauri said.

Prisha didn't answer. She had asked for proof while attending one of her lectures. And it had come to her in the form of a screenshot: Zinnia's Ola ride bill from her place to Saveer's last night.

Gauri nudged Prisha. She still didn't answer. She picked up her phone and typed something. Then she paused and typed something again. 'I'm meeting Saveer at his place in the evening.' She kept her phone down and wiped her tears with a tissue.

* * *

Prisha was sitting quietly in Saveer's living room. A man was collecting his blood sample. He was getting his blood tested as per the doctor's advice. His urine sample had already been submitted. The pathology lab guy first dabbed a wad of cotton dipped in spirit on Saveer's arm where he had located a vein, then inserted a syringe and drew out the blood. Throughout the process, Saveer and Prisha kept looking at each other. Once the man left, after informing him that he would get his reports in a day, Saveer came close to Prisha and asked, 'Now will you tell me what the problem is? I know there is something.'

'Did Zinnia come here last night?' Prisha started without a prelude.

'Zinnia? What is it about her? You've asked earlier as well.'

'Just answer me, Saveer.'

'No, she didn't come here. In fact, I haven't seen her for a long time now. What next?'

'This!' Prisha tapped on Zinnia's chat window and handed over her phone to him. Saveer played the voice note and frowned.

'What does this mean?' he asked.

'What does this mean? Really? It means what she told me. That she was here last night. And the rest of it as well!'

'She was here last night? In my house?' Saveer sounded genuinely surprised. It irked Prisha even more.

'I have a screenshot of her Ola drop receipt as well. There's no reason she would make a fool proof plan for a lie. So, I want you to tell me whatever is going on. I promise you I won't ask you any questions in return.' Prisha seemed to be on the verge of tears.

'The truth is I was alone at home last night. And I was sleeping. There is nothing more that I know of. But unfortunately, I don't have a screenshot or anything else to prove it,' Saveer said, standing up. Prisha didn't react.

'I'm sure the person who had pushed you off the edge, is doing all this to break us up,' Saveer said.

'But how could he fuck Zinnia in your house when you were there! This has happened not once but twice. I'll be honest with you, Saveer. My heart doesn't want to accept it but my mind is saying the opposite. And I'm feeling pathetic. Give me one reason, any reason. How could this be possible when you were in the house? Zinnia comes here, gets fucked by someone and you don't know about it? In fact, even Zinnia is sure that it was you!'

'Just like you were when you had come to my house once and gotten involved with someone?'

'I had not seen the face so . . .' Prisha didn't complete the sentence. She realized she hadn't asked Zinnia a very simple, obvious but pertinent question. She immediately called her up. Zinnia picked up the call after the fourth ring. Saveer gestured her to put the call on speaker. Prisha did.

'Hi, Zin, I wanted to know something really important,' Prisha said.

'Look, I'm really sorry for . . .'

'I don't have time for all that, Zin. Just tell me . . . did you see Saveer's face on the two occasions that you were here?'

There was silence at the other end. Prisha looked at Saveer in anticipation.

'A lot of things are at stake here, Zin. So, take your time but please answer honestly,' Prisha said.

'No, I didn't,' Zinnia said. 'I was blindfolded both the times. And I was commanded. I heard him though. But . . .'

That was enough for Prisha.

'Thanks. I will call you later,' she cut the call and stood up. She almost jumped up on him and hugged him tight. So tight that her soul could have transplanted on to his and their bodies wouldn't have known.

'I'm sorry, Saveer,' she whispered. He hugged her equally tightly.

'Don't be. I have a feeling that there are many such battles coming up, which we will have to win before we nab the bastard behind all this. This had to be a manipulation on his part.'

'I'm sure. He knows what happened between Utkarsh and me. And tried to do same thing with you and I.'

'I have thought a lot since our road trip. I think someone is trying to steal my identity.'

'Steal your identity?' Prisha half broke the embrace to look at him. He nodded.

'The only thing which isn't adding up is . . . why would he go on for twenty-five years.'

They remained quiet. After an hour, Prisha left. Saveer accompanied her to her two-wheeler. They didn't know that they were under the scanner.

The person who had been living in the apartment opposite Saveer's bungalow, on rent for some years now, drew the curtain after seeing Prisha drive off. The person went to a table in the room where a glass of blended Scotch was kept. Taking a sip, the person switched on the front camera of a mobile phone, muttering while posing for a selfie, 'Such a liar you are, little one. If there has been an identity theft, then it was my identity which was stolen. I was, am and will be Saveer Rathod. And you shall always be a fraudster. A fucking fraudster.'

The person clicked the selfie and was happy after checking it. It wouldn't require any filter. She was looking that good in it.

13

When Prisha reached her flat, she found Zinnia waiting for her.

'Look, I don't want to spoil our relationship over a guy,' Zinnia said the moment Prisha entered. She was surprised when Prisha hugged her and whispered in her ears, 'It's okay. You didn't fuck Saveer.'

'What!'

The way Zinnia exclaimed aroused Gauri's curiosity.

'What happened?' she asked.

'It wasn't Saveer you fucked, Zin. Now, don't freak out. Even I was fingered by the same person.'

'I wasn't fingered. I was fucked by a good, hard dick,' Zinnia said. Gauri's eyes widened. Prisha didn't have an answer. Except for the deaths in Saveer's family, she narrated whatever she knew to Gauri and Zinnia.

'Damn, we are amidst a thriller plot! I always wanted to be a part of something like this,' Gauri exclaimed.

'Shut up. This is serious. I was pushed off the hill because of my proximity to Saveer.'

'What the fuck! This is scary. Are all our lives in danger?' Zinnia asked.

'No. Only mine.' Prisha said.

There was a momentary silence.

'I'm a little scared. Can I stay with you guys tonight?' Zinnia asked.

'Of course,' Prisha said. 'But I wanted to ask you something, Zin.'

'What is it?'

'If it was really Saveer, would you have told me or continued fucking him behind my back?'

Zinnia was quiet.

'Please be honest even if it's brutal,' Prisha added.

'I don't think I would have told you,' Zinnia answered softly. Few seconds later, she added, 'It's just that Saveer is . . .'

'One helluva guy,' Prisha completed the sentence for her.

Zinnia nodded in agreement.

'And such guys always have multiple women trying to mark them their own. Just like helluva women have multiple suitors,' Gauri joined in, making the conversation further awkward.

'I'll freshen up now,' Prisha said, getting up.

Next day in college, Karthik approached Gauri while the latter was sipping tea with Prisha at Nandini's. He asked Gauri out for a movie over the weekend. She skilfully shifted the plan over to the next weekend. He agreed. He asked for her number. It seemed to Prisha that he had asked for it earlier as well. But Gauri told him she would give it to him if she enjoyed the movie. He flashed a smile and went away.

'You guys haven't exchanged numbers yet?' Prisha asked.

'Nope. But we will,' Gauri said matter-of-factly.

'Tell me one thing honestly: are you interested?'

'How many times do I need to tell you?' Gauri sounded irritated.

'As many times as I feel you are toying with him.'

'Well, I'm not. I have a grudge against the concept of love, thanks to Sanjeev. And I shall take it out on Karthik because he approached me. We all carry either the unfulfilled desires or the bottled-up grudges of our last relationships and unload them on the current ones. And many of us term this emotional relay race love. Who knows? Maybe Saveer too is living the unfulfilled desires of his last incomplete relationship and calling it love.'

'Please talk for yourself,' Prisha said, sounding hurt.

'All right, I will destroy Karthik and shall be happy if he calls it love. That's the moral he will associate with love when he gets into another relationship. Call me a bitch but that's me.'

'I know you are not. So don't pretend like one.'

'Whatever! And I'm sorry for mentioning Saveer. I'm off to the lecture.'

Prisha knew that Gauri wasn't mean. Few things provoked her into being rude although she never meant it. And the topic of love was certainly one of them. Though Prisha too attended the lecture, she couldn't get Gauri's words out of her mind. During her next break, she looked for Karthik and found him in the library. She excused herself and asked him if he could talk to her for a few minutes. Karthik recognized Prisha but he didn't know her name.

'You are Gauri's friend, right?' he said.

'Prisha.' She shook hands with him.

'Karthik.'

'I know. I just wanted to tell you something.'

'Sure.'

'In fact, I want to ask you something first.'

Karthik asked her to go on.

'Do you love Gauri or is it just casual dating that you are looking for?'

'If it was casual then I wouldn't have approached her so many times. I don't know about love but I want to know her.'

'That'll do. So, what I wanted to tell you is that she is an amazing girl but a difficult one as well. Just hang on in there. Okay?'

'Yeah, okay. I'm ready to hang on.'

'Cool. Take care.' Prisha felt better after meeting Karthik. She knew Gauri needed someone who genuinely cared for in her life even though she wasn't really in mood for that person.

Prisha called Saveer right after college. He was at home. They decided to meet there. Prisha went straight to his place and found him immersed in deep thought, holding a piece of paper as he opened the door for her.

'What happened?'

'The medical reports are in. There are heavy traces of a sleep-inducing drug in my urine sample,' he said, closing the door behind her.

'Oh! You were right. You were drugged!'

'We were drugged the other night when we camped by the backwater. And every other night when I felt too sleepy.'

'And the night when I couldn't remember being dropped off to my place,' Prisha said.

'Right. Which means . . .'

'He has access to this place?' Prisha read Saveer's mind.

'Yes. He has been living with me without my knowing it.'

Prisha had goosebumps. 'Why do I have a bad feeling about this?'

'Don't worry. I've already taken care of it. He won't be able to come inside any more. Not without being seen.'

Prisha frowned. Saveer held her hand.

'Come with me.'

He took her to the small room attached to his bedroom, which he had been using as a store room so far. A computer console was set up with a screen. Saveer picked a remote next to the monitor and pressed a button on it. The room lit up and the computer screen came alive. The screen was divided into sections, showing different parts of the house. Prisha sat in front of the screen and saw the bedroom, the washroom, the main gate, the main entrance, the hall room, the kitchen, and even the store room itself.

'This is awesome,' she said with a mischievous smile as she focused on the washroom.

'What?' Saveer shrugged.

'I can be here when you take a bath,' she said, blushing.

'*Ahan*! But why would you when we could be doing it together?' He came close to her and rubbed his face on her ears and sucked on her earlobes for a while.

'You know, I had come across a term on Google while I was researching on how to give the perfect blowjob,' Prisha whispered. Saveer smiled and whispered back, 'And what is it?'

'DIY porn. Do-it-yourself porn. Lovers record their lovemaking for later viewing,' Prisha said. There was a naughty smile on her face.

'The last time I met someone she was supposed to be only twenty.'

'But with the skillset of an adult,' she winked and stood up. She pushed Saveer on to a chair and knelt down on the floor, parting his legs a little while looking at him. He knew what was going to happen next. And it aroused him more. By the time, Prisha tugged down his pants, he had a full-blown erection. She rubbed his penis while he pressed some buttons on the remote. She turned to look at the screen. Now she could see only the two of them as captured by the CCTV in the room. She knew it was getting recorded in some master hard disk. As she looked up, the camera angle made her feel as if someone was watching them getting intimate.

'You know I had this secret fantasy of wanting to be watched while having sex,' she said.

'Really?'

Prisha nodded, 'You think he would be watching us now? Hearing us now?'

Saveer shrugged, closing his eyes as he felt her thumb on the tip of his penis.

'If he is watching or listening, then do you know what I want to tell him?' Prisha asked.

Saveer nodded, eyes still closed, enjoying the way his balls were being softly squeezed.

'Tell me,' he managed to mumble.

'I'll tell him to feel this fire which we can feel and dare him to extinguish it if he can,' Prisha said and stood up, tugging down her denim shorts and her panty. She straddled Saveer and started kissing him passionately.

While Saveer kissed her back and held her butt, she started riding him. He wasn't surprised at how wet she was. Their need was so urgent and strong that they both had absolutely nothing else on their minds.

As Prisha kept riding Saveer, approaching the zenith of lust, passion, and love, a woman standing under a fused lamp post right outside Saveer's bungalow removed her earphones. She wasn't interested in the sound of their fornication. As she walked towards her apartment, she thought: *finally, after twenty-five years, you have scored with those CCTVs. They may keep me out of your house but not out of your life. Now wait till I score back. And big.*

14

They were still in the store room. A little sweaty and cuddling together. They were done with the chair. Saveer had brought the furry mat from the living room and was sitting on it, his back against the wall with Prisha in his arms; naked. They were watching their lovemaking footage on the monitor. After it got over, Prisha turned and gave Saveer a prolonged kiss. 'I had never imagined myself in that act,' she finally said.

'Nor had I.' Saveer moved the strand of hair falling on her face.

'It's weird to see your naked self doing these things, no?'

'Why weird? I enjoyed it. In fact, I too had this on my mind for a long time but it was never possible with Ishanvi,' he said.

Prisha's body stiffened a bit with the mention of Ishanvi. She looked ahead of her and asked, 'Did you ever ask her for it?'

'No. But you know a person when you stay with him or her. She was more into subtlety.'

So, you are fulfilling desires which you had before but couldn't experience with your ex, Prisha thought. 'Can I ask you something?'

'When someone as close as you says can-I-ask-you-something, it's obvious that that something will be serious,' Saveer said jocularly.

Prisha didn't smile.

'What do you think about unfulfilled desires from a past relationship? Where do they go when the relationship ends for whatsoever reason? Or do they go away at all?'

Saveer rested his head against the wall, lost in thoughts. Suddenly, his memories of Ishanvi came gushing back. Before those clouds of memories could hit his emotional mountain, he chose to divert them by saying, 'They haunt you till you come to terms with the impossibility of those desires.'

'And how does one come to terms with something like that?'

'When new desires take over. With the arrival of a new person. A summer, a winter or a spring can never transpire the same desire as the other can in you.'

'But what if both were summers? Or winters? Or springs?'

'Are you trying to squeeze out an answer from me which is already in your head?' Saveer kind of caught her.

Prisha turned and looked into Saveer's eyes. 'I will ask you two more questions. Is what you feel with me as strong as what you felt with Ishanvi?'

'You have both given me a reason to live.'

'Isn't there anything that I alone make you feel? Which no one else ever did?'

Saveer stared at her for some time. He was about to touch her face when Prisha stopped him.

'Just answer me,' she said.

'You made me feel that a beginning is always possible. After Ishanvi's death, I had resigned from life. And I was happy not living it because I blamed myself for whatever had happened in my life, believing that I probably deserved it all. That's till you happened to me. Hope had become a corpse till you breathed fresh air into it by your presence.'

Prisha kissed his cheeks and hugged him. The slight shudder of her body told him that she was crying.

'I don't know what it is. Every moment, I feel like life will snatch you away from me and at the same time, I feel like nothing can come between us. The simultaneous surety and insecurity creates a contradiction in me which I don't know how to negate.'

'Whoever said loving someone was easy,' Saveer whispered in her ears.

'You must be thinking I'm jealous of Ishanvi, right?'

'I never thought of it that way.'

'Then you must. I'm jealous of her because she was the first one to get what is mine.

Saveer began to laugh but Prisha clamped his mouth shut with her hand.

'Don't you dare laugh. I'm dead serious.'

He removed her hand and said, 'All right, I won't laugh but allow me to take this jealous girl to the shower. We are sweating like pigs.'

'For that you don't need my permission,' she said and clung to him. He stood up, stark naked, holding Prisha and headed for the shower.

The next day in college, Prisha sat copying some notes of the previous semester from Gauri's notebooks. She had to sit for both the semester exams together and she knew it would be nothing short of a daunting task.

'Hey!' someone said. Prisha looked up to find Karthik.

'Hey!' she said.

'I'm sorry if I'm disturbing you.'

'It's okay. What's up?' Prisha said. There was a certain innocence about him that she found comforting.

'I wanted some notes. Do you think asking Gauri would be the right thing to do?'

Prisha could have laughed her heart out. Notes were an obvious excuse to approach Gauri. And the way he said it, showed how scared he was of her. But Prisha didn't laugh. Instead she pretended to think hard about it and then said, 'I think you should. Just don't be this obvious that you don't give a fuck about the notes else she would get your ass.'

Karthik smiled at her nervously. At that moment, Prisha got a call from Gauri. She picked it up.

'Where are you? My lecture is over,' Gauri said.

'I can see you. Just turn around,' Prisha said and waved at Gauri.

'All right, I'll do the needful,' he said and scampered off in another direction.

Gauri sat down beside Prisha and asked, 'What was he doing with you?'

'He was asking for some first semester notes. Told him I'll give him,' Prisha added the last part deliberately.

'Hmm. So, what's the plan? I don't feel like attending any more lectures. Are you done with your notes?'

'Almost. I'll do the rest at home.'

'Then let's go and do some bowling, bro. Been long. This stupid Diggy has also gone mad these days.'

'Did he tell you anything else about that woman?' Prisha said, arranging her stuff and standing up.

'Nothing. Don't know what spell the woman has cast on him!'

'Happens.'

As the two girls were about to catch an autorickshaw outside college, Gauri turned to Prisha and said, 'I'll give the notes to Karthik. You are anyway busy with so much work.'

Before she could say anything, Gauri hailed an autorickshaw. Prisha stood there for a few seconds with a smile on her face. She now knew that the toughness that

Gauri had been projecting was only a façade. Karthik had already reached the soft spot within her.

* * *

Diggy was at home. He had told Gauri that he wasn't feeling well. But the real reason was that the woman, who had taken his senses by storm in just a couple of meetings, had asked him for a video call. In the evening, he sat down on his bed and logged into Skype. Seconds later, his newfound ladylove called him. Diggy had never found anyone as magnetic as her to date. And the cryptic manner in which she talked would keep him on his toes all the time. Never before had anyone occupied his mind so much.

'Nice to see you, Diggy,' she said. She always talked in a low voice as if she was afraid of someone hearing her.

'Nice to see you too, ma'am,' Diggy said. His excitement was evident. She had told him not to address her as ma'am. But Diggy couldn't help it. It came out involuntarily every time he saw her.

'I'm sorry, ma'am. I think I'll need some more time to not say it.'

The woman laughed gently.

'You know why I like you, Diggy?'

Diggy shook his head.

'Because you are abnormal.'

Diggy didn't know how to react. It had been some time since someone had made him aware of his alopecia.

'Tell me, do you think you are abnormal?' the woman asked.

Diggy nodded.

'Why?'

'Because . . .' Diggy was trying to frame his answer, 'because it's not normal to not have eyebrows, hair . . .'

'That's because the majority have it. And you don't. That's how we decide what's normal and what's abnormal. But have you ever thought about the things people do behind closed doors? What about those closeted stuff? You will be amazed. When you take those things into account, there won't be any normal-abnormal business because when stripped down to our basic instincts, we are all the same. We are all predatory. Be it emotionally or sexually. An adult feeling sexually aroused by a four-year-old kid. How do you define that? Is that normal? And what about its implication? Are you getting what I'm trying to say?'

Diggy answered after a few seconds, 'Yeah, of course, yeah.'

The woman laughed again, this time a little harder.

'I know you didn't get anything. But do you want to?'

'I sure do. It will be great to gain more knowledge,' Diggy said, although he had no idea what he meant by that.

'Come to my place around 8 p.m. today and bring your laptop with you.'

'Sure.' Before Diggy could say anything else, the woman disconnected the call. He sighed deeply.

He wanted to look his best. And he did. It was when he was trying to look for a perfume inside Gauri's wardrobe that the girls arrived.

'What are you doing?' Gauri asked. Prisha was in the living room, on a call with Saveer.

Diggy gave her a caught-red-handed look.

'I'm looking for a perfume.'

'I don't have men's perfume. Don't you know you shouldn't touch a girl or open her wardrobe without her permission? Did you go to the market?' she said, pushing him away from the wardrobe.

'I know, but I just need something to smell good as I don't have anything,' Diggy said. He ignored Gauri's question.

'Why? Don't tell me you are going out on a date with that elderly woman?' Gauri sounded sardonic.

'Don't you talk to me that way!' Diggy had had enough of Gauri's mood swings. If an older woman could talk to him properly, so could she.

'Don't you touch my stuff then without my permission,' Gauri shot back.

'I don't give a damn about your stuff! And I don't need your perfume.' Diggy dashed out of the room.

'Who is giving you my perfume anyway?' Gauri yelled after him.

Diggy ran out of the house and banged the main door shut. Prisha put Saveer on hold to find out what had caused the commotion.

'What happened?'

'That woman is eating the BC's head. I've never seen him behaving like this before.'

'But where did he go?' Prisha asked.

'To hell!' Gauri yelled. She didn't know yet that she was right.

15

Hi!
Hey, not studying? It was Saveer's response to Prisha's WhatsApp message.

Nope, you free? Video call? She had a sudden urge to see him.

All right.

Prisha's face lit up. She called up Saveer immediately. Her smile only grew wider when she saw him. He had placed the phone on top of the pillows in front of him and was sitting with his back against the head of the bed. Prisha was lying on her bed holding the phone at a little distance from her.

'How come you are free? You said you were going to study?' Saveer said.

Prisha loved it when he showed concern for her academics. A man's concern towards a girl's future is immensely sexy. Especially of someone she was incorrigibly in love with.

'Gauri and Diggy had a fight. He went out,' she said.

'Where?'

'He has a date probably. That's what Gauri guessed. I think so too.'

'Diggy is dating? That's nice.'

'Yeah. Anyway, what's up with you? Had dinner?'

'Yeah.'

'And you aren't feeling sleepy-sleepy?'

'Thankfully, no. I know why you are asking though,' Saveer said.

'I was wondering if only you and I know about the CCTVs in your house. He wouldn't know anything about it unless he came to your house, right? And if he hasn't, then does he know about it already? But how?' Prisha thought aloud. She knew there were too many questions. And perhaps Saveer didn't have answers to all of them.

'I was thinking about the same. My food hasn't been spiked since our little road trip. And there's nothing much we can do till he decides to come here. It's only if and when he does that, can we involve the police as we would have some evidence.'

'Exactly!' Prisha said. There were a few seconds of silence as both were lost in their thoughts.

'Anyway,' Prisha said, 'What else? I don't like the fact that we talk so much about him. I mean we don't even know the person.'

'I know. Chuck it for the time being. You know I stumbled upon some old family photo albums. I was checking those photos before you pinged.'

'Really? I want to see them too. How did my monster look like when he was a kid?'

Saveer held up a few old photographs in front of the camera for Prisha to see.

'You have your dad's eyes and your mother's smile,' Prisha said.

'I know. The best of both,' Saveer said and smiled.

'What are our best features?' Prisha asked.

'Does that in any which way mean that you will be breeding soon?' Saveer had a naughty smile.

'Depends on you,' Prisha winked.

'Oh, come on! I don't want to breed a girl who isn't even twenty-one.'

'I'm twenty now! One year is nothing!'

'Ahem! We are not discussing this right now,' Saveer said, feeling a little conscious.

'I so like it when you are conscious. It's so opposite to your usual confident self,' Prisha blew him a kiss. Saveer blushed a bit: a first.

'OMG! Someone's blushing!'

'Come on! Give me a break, will you?'

Prisha laughed and said, 'Remember what I had told you once when I was drunk? I can give you a kid if . . .'

'Stop it! I remember very clearly.'

Prisha giggled and said, 'Okay, tell me one thing.'

'What?'

'If we have babies together then what should be the permutation-combination of their features?'

'If?' Saveer said teasingly.

'When we have babies . . .'

Saveer laughed.

'You tell me . . .' he said.

'Okay, if it's a girl then I want her to be entirely like you.'

'Entirely? Why?'

'Then she would have the good sense of choosing someone as amazing as me.'

'Yeah, sure!'

Prisha stopped laughing and said, 'I saw almost everyone from your family but how did your brother look? Don't tell me he was more handsome than you? I might just fantasize about him then!'

Saveer showed her his middle finger. Prisha laughed.

'I don't have a single picture of him, actually,' Saveer said. Prisha could see him flipping through the album.

'Not a single one? I wish you did. In fact, I so wish he was alive. I would have made you jealous for sure,' she said.

'On a serious note, I too wish he was there by my side. Sibling love, I guess, is incomparable. He left with my uncle too early, I think. And then he . . .' his voice trailed off. He looked thoughtful.

'I know. Like my sister and I have had a lot of fights but she will always be extremely special to me. I'm waiting for her to complete her boards and join me here.'

'That would be great. It will give me a chance to make you jealous, no?'

It was Prisha's time to show him the middle finger. Saveer cracked up.

'I know this may not be the right time but how did your parents die exactly? I know it must have been on one of your birthdays.'

Saveer nodded and said, 'Not on my birthday but . . .'

* * *

From Saveer's memory
His father and mother
2002 and 2005

Technically, my mother was with me longer than my father was. He died before her.

My father, Lekh Rathod, had played a crucial role in my upbringing. He taught me swimming and cycling, and cricket. He also taught me how to drive a car before I turned fifteen, and the tabla. He said he wanted me to learn everything under the sun. I always thought that he was a little too obsessed with me. Maybe after the premature death of my brother, all his hopes, aspirations and fears had started revolving around me. Not that his obsessive behaviour interfered with his parenting, except maybe on a few occasions. I remember he never allowed me to go for any outstation excursions with my classmates. I would go for outstation trips with my parents but I wasn't allowed to travel alone. I remember getting annoyed with him on such occasions. I didn't understand his paranoia; I felt angry because my friends' fathers had no problems letting their sons go on such trips.

But then, I remember sitting beside his bed in the hospital when he was struck with dengue. He looked shrivelled and fragile. He couldn't even lift his head without someone's support. I had never seen him like that. He gestured me to lean in close to him. In a cracked, rasping voice, he told me to gather as much knowledge as possible, especially before making any decision. He said certain decisions can change a person's life, can alter the course of history, can leave a lasting impact whose reverberations can be felt across time and space. Certain decisions, like a recurring nightmare, haunt the ones who make them. They cannot be dispelled, like a sin committed willingly or unwillingly. He stopped to wheeze and then added that sins catch up with the sinner sooner or later. He said guilt is the worst human emotion while repentance is the worst experience, especially for something about which nothing can be done any more. Those were his last words. He died the following morning, a week after my eighteenth birthday.

I have often wondered about the things he told me that day. But I haven't been able unravel the hidden meaning or the intention behind those words. Maybe, they were just life lessons, meant to be passed on from one generation to another. But could it be that he was guilty of something? I don't know. I would never know.

My mother, Padma Rathod, on the other hand, was less intense and more easy-going than my father. She wanted me to live my life and make my own choices, wrong or right, make mistakes and learn from them. But father didn't share her views. I often overheard them fighting over this. For the life of me, I never understood why my father was so protective of me. Maybe, they were just two very different people. In that sense, I probably had a balanced childhood. I have come across people who ask: who do you love more—mom or dad? I don't have an answer to that. How can you love one more than the other? How can you even quantify your love towards your parents? Sure, I was more comfortable with my mother, but that doesn't mean that I loved my father any less. Love is love. My mother died of cardiac arrest two years after my father's death.

I remember I had wanted to take her out that day as it was my birthday. We had planned a quiet celebration. I had gone out to fetch something. When I came back, she was standing at the doorstep, her face white as a sheet as if she had seen a ghost.

In those two years after my father's death, she had transformed into a different person. Most of the time, she seemed lost. She talked less. I don't know why. I thought she was grieving, that losing my father had snuffed out the light in her. Sometimes, she would look at me as if she had a lot to say but would never say anything. Once, however, she mentioned that certain truths are so dark that no matter how hard one tried, they could not be shared with anyone. Not even with one's family members. When I asked her to tell me clearly what she was talking about, she grew silent again, and I couldn't interpret her words.

Incidentally, neither of my parents had died on my birthday. But later, when I thought about it, I realized both were admitted to the hospital on my birthday.

16

Prisha cleared her throat. Saveer had gone into a trance while narrating the story. He gave her a forced smile.
'I'm sorry,' she said, blowing him a kiss.
'For?'
'For having taken you where you didn't want to go. I maybe young but I know what memories can do, especially the painful ones.'
'And let me tell you that the painful ones have the longest shelf life. Happy memories fade with time. You forget the details. But you remember every detail of the painful ones. I think the only thing that can really challenge time is pain.'
'I wish I was there with you right now. We would have cuddled and I'd have listened to you all night long. And then when you would've fallen asleep, I would've analysed everything you'd said. That too is a kind of love making, isn't it?'
'Sometimes you surprise me. I never imagined that your generation could be so deep.'
'There are always exceptions, sweetheart.'

'Now I know. And I'm glad that I know.' Saveer blew her a kiss over the phone.

'Oh! someone's catching up,' Prisha said. She knew how uncomfortable and awkward Saveer was with cyber display of affection.

'Talking of learning, I think you should call it a night now. And study in the morning?'

'Yeah, I'll have to.'

After ending the call, Prisha went to the kitchen, drank some water and went to the living room to check on Gauri. She had told her that she would join her in a minute. And that minute had turned into an hour with an unplanned video call with Saveer.

'Gauri?' she said softly as the lights in the living room were out. There was no response. As her eyes adjusted to the darkness, she noticed Gauri sitting in a corner, near the window, leaning against the wall.

'Gauri?' No response. Prisha switched on the lights. She went close to Gauri and realized that she had dozed off. Prisha was about to go back to her room when she noticed Gauri's phone lying beside her. She picked it up. The screen showed that a call was still on. It was Karthik.

'Okay, I am not asleep,' Gauri said. Prisha was taken aback. Before she could react, Gauri snatched the phone away from her.

'We'll talk tomorrow. Goodnight,' she told Karthik and cut the call, and went to her room.

'What the hell just happened? Why were you trying to hide the fact that you were talking to Karthik?' Prisha followed her to her room and stood next to the door, her hands on her waist.

'I didn't want you to know,' Gauri said softly.

'Know what?'

'That we have been talking at nights.'

'But why would it bother me?'

'I thought if you had got wind of it, then you'd try to convince me that it's love,' Gauri said as she got into bed. She switched on the AC and covered herself with a blanket.

'That I'll do anyway,' Prisha said, switching off the room's light and joining Gauri on the bed. She turned towards her and continued, 'But that's for later. Right now there's only one thing I want to know.'

'You scared me the way you said it.' Gauri said.

'Come on! Bros don't scare each other. What I want to know is simple—do you love Karthik?'

'I knew that was coming.'

'So, don't keep your bro waiting,' Prisha said, looking at Gauri intently.

'The answer is simple. I don't know.'

'Okay. I didn't hear that. I want a proper answer.'

'Aargh! Why are you doing this to me?' Gauri said, turning her back to Prisha and trying to sleep.

Prisha held her tight. 'Why are you doing this to yourself, Gauri? Like, why? If you like the guy, go ahead and date him. He too likes you. See how and where it goes. We don't need to take all the decisions on the first day itself.'

'I know all that but I feel the easier it is to get into a relationship, the difficult it is to come out of it.' Prisha let go of her.

'But why are you thinking about the end already?'

'Maybe because it's easier to think about the end before starting anything so as to not wonder why and how things happened.'

'But that means you're obsessed with the ending! That's not the right way of getting into a relationship.'

'I don't want this, but if you break up with Saveer then tell me honestly, would you tell this to yourself?'

Prisha was quiet. For the first time, she understood the fear that Gauri was running away from, even as a part of her wanted to get closer to Karthik.

'Your silence is my answer,' Gauri said.

Prisha lay back, staring at the ceiling. 'Between Utkarsh and Saveer, I've learnt that while some relationships seem like they'll make you, they actually end up breaking you. And some that seem to destroy you, actually end up giving you a new lease of life. I don't think anyone can know what will happen until they choose to be in a relationship.'

'I agree. And that's why I am taking baby steps towards it and not a leap or even a jump,' Gauri said.

'Hmm. I get it now. As long as it is a journey towards something you feel connected to, I guess it's fine.'

'How slow is slow and how fast is fast is the question.'

'Let the connection decide that.'

'Yeah, you are right.'

They lay silent for a while.

'By the way, any news of Diggy? He has never been out this late. Not alone, I mean,' Prisha said.

'He has never fallen for a "lady" before!' Gauri rolled her eyes. The girls laughed. Prisha nudged her, saying, 'Don't be mean.'

She called Diggy. He didn't pick up.

'Do you think the woman is fucking him?' Gauri asked.

'Stop it, will you? Your sudden weird questions bring up stupid visuals in my head,' Prisha said and messaged him: *call back, moron.* She kept the phone beside her pillow and went to sleep.

When she opened her eyes, she thought her alarm had woken her up. Then she realized it was the shrill ringtone of her phone. Someone was calling her. She picked it up with half-closed eyes. It was Saveer. She took the call, but before she could say anything, Saveer said something in one breath. She sat upright in bed, wide awake.

17

Prisha disconnected the call and woke up Gauri, shivering.

'What happened? I'll get up a little later,' Gauri said groggily and turned over.

'Something has happened to Diggy,' Prisha said. Her voice was shaking.

'What?' Gauri rubbed her eyes.

'Something bad has happened to Diggy,' Prisha repeated. 'We need to rush.'

The girls wasted no time in getting ready. They took a cab straight to Saveer's place but he called Prisha midway.

'Have you seen the nursing home near my place? The one on the right when you take a left for my lane?'

Prisha remembered.

'Yes.' She was finding it difficult to speak. Her mind was racing

'I'll meet you there,' he said.

Prisha spotted Saveer right outside the nursing home gate. He was standing next to a police van and a jeep.

'Where's Diggy?' Gauri asked the moment she got out the cab.

'He is in the ICU.'

Gauri dashed inside. Prisha was about to follow suit when Saveer held her hand.

'He is no more,' Saveer said softly. Prisha stopped dead in her tracks. Saveer released her hand but she nearly collapsed.

'What . . . What do you mean?'

'I didn't tell you over the phone. Diggy was raped and thrown outside my house. Dead.'

'He was what?' Prisha couldn't believe what she had just heard.

'Raped.'

Prisha was about to say something when an emotionally dishevelled Gauri stumbled out of the nursing home. She came straight towards Prisha and held her tight, sobbing uncontrollably.

'Diggy isn't saying anything, Prisha. That moron is quiet like a log. What the fuck is wrong with him?' Gauri hid her face in Prisha's bosom and sobbed loudly. Fat tears rolled down Prisha's cheeks as well as she tried to console Gauri.

'Take care of her. I will need Diggy's parents' phone number. We need to inform them. The police are inside,' Saveer said.

It took Prisha a few minutes before she could coax Gauri into give Diggy's parents' number to her. Saveer saved the number on his phone and went inside.

Prisha and Gauri were allowed to see the body but only for a few minutes. It was then sent for postmortem and a forensic examination. His family was informed by the police. They were on their way from Indore.

While the two girls went home, totally distressed, Saveer went to the police station to check the CCTV footage of outside his house. Around 3.31 a.m., a hatchback car was seen stopping right outside Saveer's house. It had a car-cover except on the left side, from where the body was pushed out. Neither the model nor the number plate of the car was visible.

'Why your house, Mr Rathod?' asked the officer in charge, Vijay Shetty.

'I don't have any idea,' Saveer said. His lawyer, M.K. Kumaraswamy, had joined him at the police station.

'It could be a coincidence. I don't think my client is linked to the case at all. Just that the deceased's flatmate is his girlfriend. That can't be the reason for interrogating him.'

'I was only asking a simple question,' Shetty clarified, maintaining his poise. 'It isn't an interrogation. I've known Mr Rathod for a long time. He has been doing a really good job with G-Punch.'

'It's okay,' Saveer told Kumaraswamy. The word 'coincidence' brought back flashes of the deaths in his family. He hoped that it wasn't what was going on in his mind. The police and the lawyer may not be able to figure out the link but it seemed like a direct message to him.

Who is this goddamn person? Saveer clenched his fist in frustration. With a lot of effort, he calmed himself down and turned to Shetty. 'I'll have to leave,' he said.

'Certainly.'

'Please keep me updated on this. My girlfriend and Diggy were very close. And at any point if you have a query, please feel free to contact me.'

'Of course, I will. Thank you, Mr Rathod.'

Saveer and Kumaraswamy left the police station. Once outside, Saveer called up Prisha. She was still at home with Gauri. Saveer drove to her place. While driving, he kept trying to convince himself that he had done the right thing by not telling the police about the strange sequence of events ever since he had started dating Prisha, or for that matter since he was ten years old. *What if the person tries to commit another heinous crime like this, that is if he has really killed Diggy? But rape?* It was something even Saveer couldn't digest.

The girls had cried their eyes out by the time Saveer reached. The door was open. He sat down beside them in the living room. He didn't know how to initiate a conversation. He had lost many loved ones, so he knew that at such a time one has a lot to say but also want to stay quiet. It is a difficult situation when one part of you is in denial and the other has accepted the harsh truth.

After a few minutes, Gauri said, 'Prisha said Diggy was raped. Is that true?'

'Initial investigation suggests so. But there were no traces of semen.'

'There won't be any. It's a woman who raped Diggy!' Gauri said. Saveer looked at her incredulously and then at Prisha. The latter nodded.

'How do you know?'

'Diggy was going mad about this woman who was apparently amazingly beautiful,' Prisha said, 'In fact, he was behaving stupidly of late because of her. He was so smitten.'

'Who is this woman? Where does she live? Do you guys have her number?'

Both Gauri and Prisha looked at him blankly.

'Nothing at all?'

'Maybe we can get it from his phone?' Prisha said.

'The police haven't found his phone yet. The number is switched off,' Saveer said, sounding thoughtful. A few seconds passed.

'Are you thinking what I am thinking?' Prisha asked Saveer and they looked at each other intently.

'But the motive?' Saveer asked.

'Us? He wants to tell us that if we don't stop, he will toy with us like this. By killing the people we love.'

'What are you guys talking about?' Gauri looked at both of them, alarmed.

'Didn't you tell her?' Saveer asked.

'Tell me what!'

Prisha sighed. Gauri only knew about her being pushed off at Nandi Hills, nothing else. She took a few seconds to brace herself. The shock of Diggy's death was still riding heavily on her. Once she felt a little in control, Prisha told her what had happened at Nandi Hills on Saveer's birthday—that there was someone out there who had killed everyone who had come close to Saveer. And that Prisha was the only one who had survived the attempt made on her life.

'I don't believe this!' Gauri sounded shocked.

'It is a bit outlandish but is true nevertheless,' Prisha said. She went on to tell her about her encounters, and also those of Zinnia's, about the man with a voice similar to that of Saveer's. In all probability, he was perhaps the murderer, who had used the alias of a woman.

'But Diggy said she was a woman. He wasn't stupid to have mistaken a man for a woman!' Gauri exclaimed.

'That's why I doubt if it's a *him*. But then, why would a woman rape Diggy? Is such a thing even possible?' Prisha said.

'It is a *him*. I know this because leaving the body right in front of my house couldn't have been a coincidence. It simply couldn't. Saveer grew agitated.

'All our doubts will be cleared once the person is caught,' Prisha said.

'What I want to know is: did you know all along that people who come close to you, die?' Gauri asked Saveer.

She looked him in the eye, not giving him an opportunity to duck the question.

'Yes, I did.'

'Then why didn't you tell Prisha about it! What if she had died after falling off the cliff at Nandi Hills? Who would have been blamed?'

My weak and selfish self didn't let me confess, Saveer thought but didn't say anything.

'Gauri, it's okay,' Prisha said.

'I'm sorry but this is not okay! I would have lost you because of him. I have lost Diggy because of him. He has no right to destroy us like this. So what if he loves you?' the pitch of her voice was rising every second.

'Gauri, shut up!' Prisha sensed that the discussion was on the verge of becoming an argument.

'He should explain. Or just butt off from your life. If it really is the person who has been killing all his loved ones, then he will kill me too one day. Will you be okay then as well?' This time it was Prisha's turn to answer.

'I'm sorry, Saveer. She isn't in her senses.'

'I'm perfectly in my senses. Mr Saveer Rathod, could you care to explain what your plan of action is regarding this, apart from just waiting and watching us getting killed? And who knows, raped as well?'

'Gauri!' Prisha almost screamed.

Saveer stood up.

'I'll call you soon.' He left.

Saveer didn't call Prisha that night. Nor did he take her calls. She called him a few times, after which he messaged her saying he was busy with some office project. Prisha understood that Gauri's words had not gone down well with him. But she couldn't even blame her. Gauri was right. It was just that Prisha didn't have a solution. Nor did Saveer.

Diggy's parents reached Bengaluru the next day. By then, Gauri had told Prisha what Diggy never had— the love of his family. His parents had always shunned him because of his condition. They had sponsored his education in a residential school and later in a college, but maintained their distance. Prisha couldn't digest the fact.

'A lot of shit goes on in this world. And we keep our eyes closed for far too many of them,' Gauri said.

Diggy had an elder brother and a younger sister. They didn't come. His parents stayed at a hotel and came to collect Diggy's belongings. They cried but Prisha could tell it was hogwash.

Even when Diggy's body was released to be cremated, they didn't bother taking it back to Indore. They simply cremated it in Bengaluru. Prisha and Gauri joined them. As his body was carried away, Prisha understood what her parents must have gone through when she was in the hospital. And then a disturbing thought struck her. *What if Gauri was killed next?*

Prisha knew that Saveer was right when he had said that leaving the body in front of his house was no coincidence. The statement that the person playing this dirty game was making was also clear: If you two don't break up, then more people will die.

Diggy's parents left for the airport with their son's ashes. They asked the girls to keep the two-wheeler with them. Prisha and Gauri rode back to their apartment with heavy hearts. Neither of them had attended college since Diggy's death.

'Isn't it possible that Diggy was raped by someone else after he met the woman?' Prisha asked as they were riding back home.

'Are you saying it's a random rape? In India, guys don't get so randomly raped on the streets at night. Especially, in a metropolis like Bengaluru,' Gauri slowed down a bit.

'I am not saying that. What if the woman Diggy was so suddenly crazy about has nothing to do with it? Maybe the person who attacked me at Nandi Hills is behind the murder.'

'You mean that person is gay? Like he is obsessed with Saveer and hence kills anyone who loves him or the ones he loves?'

'But then he could have simply killed Diggy, why rape and kill him?' Prisha sounded as if she was asking herself the question.

'Don't mind my saying this, Prisha, but do you really think Saveer is worth all this? More than your life? You have your parents, your sister, me. You were pushed off a bloody hill for fuck sake! Your parents don't know that else they would have never allowed you to stay back in Bengaluru.'

Prisha knew that she was right.

'I would not only suggest but also request you to call it quits with Saveer, however distressing it may be. I don't know what you were thinking when you went back to him after nearly dying,' Gauri said.

What was I thinking? Prisha wondered. She had only one thing in mind—she loved Saveer. Saveer loved her back. And she was confident that when two people loved each other genuinely then a lot of shit can be taken care of. But . . . What if people start dying?

Prisha placed her head on Gauri's shoulder, hoping some magic would happen and her love story with Saveer wouldn't be compromised. Both of them remained quiet even after they reached their flat. Diggy's room was empty. His laptop had been missing since his death. Gauri logged in to Facebook on her phone and started going through Diggy's pictures. Prisha simply lay on the bed, trying to think through everything. It was around nine in the night when her phone rang, flashing Saveer's name. It had been a few days since they had spoken, communicating only through texts. Prisha took the call immediately.

'Hi!'

'Hi, Prisha. I'm sorry but I'll need some time of yours. Are you free?'

He sounded unnaturally formal.

'Yes, but what has happened?' Prisha's voice sounded brittle.

'I'm coming over to your place in some time. Let's go for a drive. We need to talk.'

Prisha had a bad feeling about it.

18

Prisha stood at the window, looking out for Saveer's car. She had an inkling of what Saveer might say but she wasn't ready to accept it. She kept telling herself it was something related to Diggy's death. Maybe some clue had emerged? Her heart skipped a beat when she saw his car screech to a halt near her apartment gate. Her phone rang.

'Yeah, I'm coming down in a minute,' she said. She took a deep breath and thought: *please god, let this not be what I think it is going to be*.

Gauri had fallen asleep, so Prisha locked the door from outside and went downstairs. Saveer greeted her coldly, which made her more nervous. She sank into her seat and put the seat belt on as Saveer drove out of the lane.

It was late in the night and the roads were mostly empty.

'What is it, Saveer? I can't bear the silence any more,' Prisha said.

'When I had first felt something for you, I had fought hard but failed to follow my instinct to not get involved with you. I failed to listen to my instinct even after you were released from the hospital. I shouldn't have continued but . . .'

'But you did.'

'Yes. I did. Hoping against hope that things would stay normal.'

Changing the gear, he took a turn rather abruptly. Prisha gripped her seat to steady herself.

'But finally, I have accepted it. It can't be normal. I can never be in a relationship. Gauri was right. When I know what the consequences are, I don't have the right to involve myself with anyone. After all, I'm risking another person's life. In the last twenty-five years, there has been no attempt made on my life.'

'And yet you have died every day in those last twenty-five years.'

'Yes, I have.' Saveer stopped the car. Prisha didn't know where exactly they were. There was so much on her mind that she had lost track of the turns that he had taken.

'I'm ready to die, but I can't take any more deaths on my conscience,' Saveer said, switching on the parking lights and getting out of the car. It was drizzling. Prisha followed him outside. They stood on either side of the car.

Don't you understand, Saveer? Till now, you may have died every day because of all those deaths but from now onwards, if we call it quits, we will both die every day? Prisha thought. *I know, if we continue there is a possibility that my dear ones too can die but is that reason enough to separate and kill each other like no death ever will? Destroy each other like no life ever will?* Prisha looked up helplessly at the cloudy sky.

Saveer was staring at the blinking lights of a passing airplane. It was playing hide and seek with the clouds. Just like his mind was playing with his heart. *I know it's difficult for you, Prisha. It is the same with me. Certain relationships alter you when you are in it. And once they break, that alteration seems like a fairy tale. And because it seems like a fairy tale, you stop believing in the feasibility of it. You turn into the worst version of yourself. I may treasure the alteration, but I won't ever go close to it again. And whoever makes me feel close to it, I will shun that person as well. I know this because I have gone through it after Ishanvi's death. But how do I explain it to you without coming across as someone who is done with this relationship. I swear I am not done.*

Prisha folded her hands and looking down at the wet tarmac. *You'd told me once about Complete Love. You made me experience it as well. And now you want to make me understand what the loss of love is. It may be just a break-up for the rest of the world, but for me it will be a loss. The pain will be far more acute than the pain of a break-up.* She tried hard not to break down, but couldn't.

Saveer glanced at her and realized that she was crying. He sighed and walked up to her. *It's all my fault, I know*, he thought, standing against the car, beside her. *If involving myself with you was a mistake to begin with, then reconnecting with you after you were released from the hospital was a blunder. Between you and I, I'm the mature one. I should have acted like one. It's not surprising where it has led us to. What is surprising is how I allowed it to reach so far, despite knowing every damn thing. Once you give in to love, I tell you, it can toy with all your maturity, mental and emotional poise and your decision-making ability.* Saveer moved a bit. Their hands brushed accidentally. Prisha looked up at him expectantly. Hot tears rolled down her cheeks. He braced himself; if he broke down, Saveer knew he wouldn't be able to steer the situation in the direction he wanted to.

'We may stand here for the rest of the night but it's not going to change anything, Prisha,' he said. Saveer knew there was no pleasant way of putting across to her what he was there for.

'This is it?' Prisha asked, almost in a whisper.

'I'm afraid, it is. We have to break up before anybody else is attacked.'

'What if I say I'm not ready for this? I never will be.'

'Trust me, we both won't ever be ready for this. We have to do this first and then allow time to prepare us for it.'

'And what if time isn't able to prepare us for it? Prepare me for it? What am I supposed to do then?'

'You are very young now. As you grow up, you'll understand what you're supposed to do about it.'

'You are a grown-up. You already know, isn't it?'

'Yeah,' Saveer said and thought, *who am I kidding?*

'Then, tell me. I also want to know.'

Saveer closed his eyes and placed his hands on his hips. He was losing grip on the conversation.

'Look, Prisha, you can continue asking questions and I will continue answering them. You don't want this to end and I . . .'

'You want this to end, Saveer?'

'I don't want this to end but I will have to end it. There's a difference. So let's just do it. We aren't meeting from tomorrow onwards. Neither in office nor outside. Please don't make it more difficult.'

'It already is more than difficult.'

'Come, let me drop you home.'

One last time, Prisha thought and said, 'Saveer, wait.'

He turned around to look at her.

'I want to hug you,' Prisha said. *One last time.*

Saveer came back to her. He was cautious not to make her feel that he was equally vulnerable. Prisha hugged him, placing her ear against his chest. She could hear his heartbeat race a tad bit faster. She closed her eyes and tried to consume the moment. The way she hugged him tighter with every passing second triggered an emotional chaos in Saveer. But before the chaos could bewitch him and provoke him into exposing his helpless self, Saveer broke the hug. They got into the car. No words were exchanged. He dropped her home and left.

When Prisha reached home, she noticed that Gauri was drunk. She had been drinking Old Monk on her own while re-living old memories with Diggy on Facebook.

'Join in,' she said.

'Saveer and I broke up,' Prisha said.

'If you had done it before then who knows, perhaps Diggy would have been alive today.'

'Thanks for the guilt trip,' Prisha said and grabbed the bottle from her. She took a few swigs. Prisha had never drunk rum neat. It burnt her throat but she gulped down some more. And some more until her senses dimmed. In the meantime, Gauri passed out while blabbering continuously. When not even a drop fell in her mouth even after inverting the bottle completely, Prisha kept it aside and stood up. She was finding it difficult to focus. And yet there was something on her mind that even her drunk self was determined about.

How can we not kiss one last time? she thought and stumbled towards the main door. I'm sure Saveer will agree too.

'We both deserve one last kiss. In fact, we owe it to each other,' she mumbled to herself as she struggled to wear Gauri's shoes thinking they were hers. She staggered her way downstairs to the main gate where the two-wheeler was parked. As she fumbled with the keys, a woman said something from behind.

'Did you say something to me?' Prisha asked.

'I asked if I may help you?' the woman, standing across the road, repeated her question.

19

'Can you? I need to go to Saveer's place,' Prisha's speech slurred. She didn't know who the woman was. She wasn't even interested.

'Sure,' the woman said. 'Do you know why I was here?'

'No. Why?'

'I had a feeling that you might do something stupid tonight.'

'Really? Do you know me?'

'A little bit. Nobody can ever know anyone well. Can they? We only think we do. Till the person betrays us and we realize how little we knew about them.'

'Take the shortcut, okay?' Prisha said.

'I know where he stays,' the woman said matter-of-factly.

'You know where he stays? Don't tell me you are one of Mean Monster's girls?' Prisha grasped the seat of the two-wheeler tightly in order to stand straight. The woman didn't react. She crossed the lane and boarded the scooty, starting the engine. Almost as if she was programmed, Prisha sat on the pillion. The woman drove off.

'Didn't you guys break up?' the woman asked.

'Yeah, we did,' Prisha said, too drunk to even wonder how the woman knew about it.

'Then why are you going to his place?'

'For one last kiss,' Prisha blabbered.

The woman scoffed. 'You love him a lot?'

'More than a lot.'

'There was a time when I too wished to experience love. I don't know if it will ever happen. Not that I wish it any more but just saying,' she said, driving slowly.

'You should experience it. It's a good thing but remember only to experience Complete Love. Like I experienced with Saveer. It's important to understand Complete Love. Only then will you know that the rest is bullshit.'

'But I've been manipulated not to experience it. Not to feel it. Not to even love the sound of it.'

'Oh! Who did that to you? In fact, why would anyone do that? This is so wrong,' Prisha said, hardly registering anything.

'The same person whose house we are driving to.'

'Saveer? He couldn't possibly do such a thing,' Prisha frowned.

'Just shows how little you know about him.'

Prisha was leaning on the woman, her head against her back and her eyes closed.

'He isn't Saveer. He is someone else,' the woman said. She was expecting a reaction. But none came. She stopped the scooty. Turning back, she found Prisha asleep. The woman managed to hold on to Prisha and took a U-turn. She drove her back to her apartment. She parked the two-wheeler next to the gate and took her upstairs. Initially, she thought of leaving her outside the flat. But when she reached upstairs, she found the door ajar. Prisha must have forgotten to lock it, she guessed, and peeped inside. There was nobody. So she dragged her inside and lay her down on the couch in the living room and left immediately.

The next morning when Prisha woke up, she had the worst hangover of her life. Gauri was still asleep. Try as she did, she could not recall what had transpired the night before. Only scenes of her break-up kept flashing in front of her eyes. She tried to go back to sleep. She had no memory of the scooter ride with the woman who had raped Diggy. And killed Saveer's family members.

The first thing Saveer did after waking up was pull out all the CCTV cameras from his house.

'There is no need for these any more,' he said out loud. 'If I have to suffer, I have to suffer. Let's not make hue and cry over it. It's been twenty-five years already. Another twenty-five years maybe.'

The last camera left was in the store room. While pulling it out, Saveer couldn't help but reminisce how Prisha and he had made love in the same room a few weeks ago. He looked at the chair and could almost hear their cries. It was one of the most passionate moments of his life. So passionate that he was convinced that he would surpass any crisis with Prisha by his side. The hangover of that day jabbed at his insides.

I have to live with it and die with it, Saveer thought, anger replacing the pain. He dumped the cameras in the garbage bin outside the main gate. Then he went back inside and deleted all the stored footage in the computer and plugged out the console. Life was back to being what it was earlier: a big zero.

In office, Saveer asked Krishna to mail Prisha and Gauri their official termination letters. He tried hard to concentrate on his work, but couldn't. In the end, he gave up and decided to hit the gym instead. After a strenuous workout, he went home and crashed early.

It was some time during the night when someone unlocked the main door of his house. A woman entered. She closed the door behind her and went upstairs to the bedroom.

Saveer was fast asleep on his bed, facing the door. She noticed the tattoo that she had inked on him as a warning to not attempt what he had been trying for years now—to gift himself happiness. It irked her.

As she walked inside the bedroom, the light on top of the bed switched on. She looked at Saveer. He looked dead. *The drug had done its work*, she thought. She had overheard him through the microphone in his cufflink about the removal of the CCTV cameras. From the house opposite his, she had even seen him dump them in the garbage bin outside. Everything was going back to how it used to be. Perhaps, from now onwards, she wouldn't have to kill anyone any more.

She sat on the edge of the bed and taking Saveer's head on her lap, caressed it like a mother. 'Good to know you have finally realized this, little one. Though it took you more than two decades, I'm happy it has finally happened. You can't escape me. Just like I can't escape you. And for me to be happy, you will have to be unhappy. I'm sorry that's the way it is,' she said softly. 'No, wait a minute,' she said, her face hardening. 'I'm not sorry. You deserve every bit of my wrath. You should feel lucky that I spared Prisha. You know why? I'm tired of killing people. I know what it is to kill innocent people. How their families have cursed me even though they didn't know who I was. But what could I have done? You left me with no choice. Prisha is a nice girl. She will come out of this bullshit-bubble of forever kind of love. There's nothing of that sort. Everything that humans do has a selfish motive. Just that we are intelligent enough to cover up and convince ourselves that the reason aren't selfish. Look at you!' The woman paused for a moment, restraining herself from digging her nails into his skin.

'Just look at you, Mr Fraudster Rathod. One cheeky bastard you are, who knows how to feel sympathetic towards his own self when he himself invited trouble with his own karma. Huh! I'm appalled how people don't see through you? You robbed me of the right to be myself. Do you understand how big an emotional crime that is? To do something so dastardly to someone, for no fault of his, that the victim never ever comes out of that trauma. It is like carrying your own corpse with you all the time. I've lost my ability to feel for others because of you. I've lost my instinct to trust others because of you. I never developed the urge to be loved by someone because of you. And I couldn't let anyone explain to me what it feels like when two bodies, wrapped in their skins and smelling of their raw fragrances, come together to experience one of the most basic activities there is. And you thought I would let you go? You wish, Mr Fraudster.' The woman placed Saveer's head back on the pillow and stood up. She sat on the rocking chair beside the bed. She had tears in her eyes. She could count the number of times she had cried in her life—there weren't many. But tonight she did. Tonight she was sure she wouldn't have to kill anyone any more. She wasn't a psychopath who revelled in someone's death. She was a human being who had been wronged. She took out her phone and switched on the front camera. She hated what she saw in the screen. And yet she knew she had to live with it. Just like the man on the bed would have to live with the fact that he had been fucked for life. She chuckled devilishly.

Saveer had put ten alarms, each fifteen minutes apart, before he had dozed off that night. Yet, he woke up late. For a moment, he sat looking around, suspecting something untoward. The digital clock on the bedside table showed 9.13 a.m. Still drowsy, he got out of bed and went to the store room. There was a ladder there, which he picked up and went to the living room. He climbed up the ladder and touched every bulb in the room. After the inspection, he was disappointed. He did the same thing in the kitchen, then in the store room and in the washroom. He came back to the living room and sat on the couch, disappointed. He frowned when he realized that he was yet to check his bedroom. Saveer rushed upstairs with the ladder. He checked all the bulbs and slowly a smile appeared on his lips. The light bulb above his bed was warm. Someone was there in the room all night, perhaps till the morning.

Saveer punched the air. *Yes! The plan had worked.* He had intentionally removed the cameras. He had hoped it would lure the person back and it had. When he had chosen to prepare his dinner with the slightly stale vegetables in the refrigerator, he had hoped they would be spiked. They were. He hoped the person would come back. He did. *But how did the person know he had uninstalled the cameras?* Saveer wondered. He would soon find out. Now it was time to act as if he didn't know anything. As if everything was how it used to be. Meanwhile, he would install a few secret cameras and wait for the person to visit him again.

'Someone will be waiting for him this time,' Saveer murmured, smirking.

20

Saveer felt a surge of excitement. He went to office but one question kept nagging him. *How did the person know that he had removed the cameras? That too so quickly.* Saveer racked his brains but couldn't think of anything. Was he being watched?

In between his meetings, Saveer asked Krishna to arrange a few micro cameras whose live feed could be seen on his phone. He also asked him to keep it strictly confidential. Saveer was itching to text Prisha about the development but held himself back. He decided to wait for some more time before reaching out to her.

Meanwhile, Saveer went about his daily routine the way he had before Prisha had come into his life. He went out alone to *Ishanvi's* for lunch and in the evening hit the gym. When he came back home, he followed the user's manual and installed the cameras himself. Saveer was careful not to install the cameras in their old locations. He was satisfied with the results—he could see the visuals clearly on his phone. As he went to the kitchen to prepare his dinner, Saveer hoped that the food would be spiked. He had ordered fresh vegetables before going to office. By now he was sure the person had a spare key and had used it to enter his house in his absence, spiked the food and . . .what did the person do after drugging him? Some unanswered questions were finally resolved— that was how he had that tattoo on his body, and that was how Prisha and Zinnia were seduced. But the real question was why? Why had the person been doing what he had been doing for all these years? Saveer had a gut feeling that he was closing in on the answer. He ate his food and waited for sleep to take over. But he didn't feel sleepy. He read, worked a bit on his laptop, even watched some television, but sleep remained elusive. Wasn't his food spiked? Nothing happened that night, or on the next two nights. Frustration started building up inside Saveer.

It was on the third day when he was in office and casually decided to check the live camera feed that his suspicion proved to be true. He had installed three cameras—one in the bedroom, one in the living room and the other in the kitchen. The bedroom and the living room were empty, but when he switched on the kitchen camera, he literally jumped from his seat. There was someone sitting on the floor with all the vegetables scattered around her. He tried to zoom in but wasn't able to. He saw the person taking one vegetable at a time and injecting something into them, especially the ones he used in his daily salads. The woman then took out the chicken from the freezer and repeated the same procedure. But for the life of him, Saveer couldn't believe that it was a woman. He had always assumed it was a man. He remembered when Prisha had told him about a woman visiting her in the hospital and warning her not to meet him. *Didn't she also say that she had almost sounded like him? Who was this woman?* Saveer stared at his phone without blinking. The woman's face wasn't visible.

Saveer watched as the woman neatly put back all the veggies and the chicken inside the refrigerator and left. He switched to the living room camera. The woman was now standing on the couch and reaching for the wall clock in the room. Saveer couldn't understand what exactly she was doing with it. The clock, as far as he knew, was working perfectly. Once she was done, she stepped down from the couch and went towards the stair case. It was clear that she was heading to the bedroom. Saveer switched to the bedroom's camera. *If only I had put the camera in its old place, I would've been able to see her face*, Saveer thought.

Inside the bedroom, the woman picked up the digital clock on bedside table. Saveer frowned. *What the hell was she doing with the clocks?* After doing something to clock, the woman left the room. Saveer switched back to the living room camera. The woman came downstairs and left the house, closing the main door behind her. Saveer tapped the live feed close. He sat back on his chair, unable to think of anything conclusive. It wasn't really about who the woman was. There was something else. He could sense it sitting in his office. Saveer touched his forehead and thought hard. What if he now informed the police, and asked them to keep an eye on the house and catch the woman the moment she tried to enter the house? A sudden smile appeared on his face. He felt a resurgence of hope. He quickly called Krishna.

'Yes, sir,' Krishna said, stepping inside the room.

'Please connect me to officer Shetty as soon as possible. Tell him I know who could have killed Digambar. And why.'

'Right, sir.'

Saveer controlled his urge to call up Prisha. *Soon!* He told himself. What he didn't know was that he had been heard by the same person he was watching a minute ago.

21

Krishna peeped inside the room and said, 'Sir, officer Shetty is on the line.'

'Hello, officer, this is Saveer.'

'Hello, Mr Rathod, tell me, how may I help you?' Shetty said.

'This may take a while so I hope you aren't busy.'

'I have time. If you want, we can meet and talk as well,' Shetty suggested.

'I can't meet you right now. I mean I can meet you but I think I am being watched.'

'Being watched?'

'That's right. And meeting you may just push me away from what I think is a proof to Digambar's murder. . .' Saveer paused.

'Go on, Mr Rathod, I'm listening.' Shetty sounded interested now.

Saveer took his time explaining the strange sequence of events. How he had assumed that the deaths were a series of coincidences till recent developments. He also told Shetty that he was convinced that a woman was behind everything: the one he saw in his house through the secret cameras. Throwing Diggy's body outside his house wasn't just a coincidence, he said, just like Prisha's fall wasn't a standalone act. Just that he still wasn't sure about the motive of the woman. Or her identity.

There was silence on the other end once Saveer was done narrating his story.

'You there, officer?' Saveer asked.

'I think this is one of the most intriguing cases of my career.'

'And the most frustrating one of my life.'

'I understand, Mr Rathod. But don't you suspect anyone? There's always someone.'

'No one at all.'

'What if she is one of the women you slept with?'

Saveer had told him about his Mean Monster phase as well. He didn't want to hide anything. There was too much at stake.

'She may have gone crazy for you or something,' Shetty suggested.

'I wasn't sleeping around since I was ten.'

'Ah, yes. But what if the earlier deaths really were coincidences while there is actually someone who pushed off your girlfriend from the cliff and killed Digambar?'

'That could explain Prisha's fall but why kill Digambar?'

There was silence.

'I guess we'll get the answers once we nab this woman who had entered your house after drugging you.'

'Exactly.'

'Could you send the video to me now?'

'Sure. My assistant, Krishna, will get it for you in a pen drive.'

'Let me call you once my team and I have watched it.'

'Thank you so much, officer.'

Saveer immediately copied the footage in a pen drive and asked Krishna to deliver it to the officer. Saveer was dying to go back home and check what the woman had done with the clocks but he controlled himself. He didn't want to do anything that might tip the woman off. Everything needed to be normal, he told himself, and got back to work.

* * *

The professor was giving a lecture on ethics in journalism. Prisha was sitting with Gauri. Though she was looking at the professor, her mind was blank. She knew she had to concentrate in class because her exams were near and she had to take two sets together. But no matter what she couldn't focus. *Normal* seemed like a distant possibility. Everyone has that one life-altering incident which changes them—the way one thinks, the outlook towards life, priorities, likes and dislikes. Her experience with Saveer had been a coming-of-age moment for her.

The professor's voice faded as Prisha thought about the past year and a half. She knew that she had grown up. The layer of innocence that had cocooned her for so long had been peeled off. She thought about how people often romanticize that which they cannot have. *Like I will be romanticizing Saveer and my relationship. It will soon, who knows maybe it has already, become an emotional benchmark for me to match all my future relationships against.* She also knew that to romanticize her relationship with Saveer would automatically result in a constant rejection of all her future relationships. They would never live up to that standard. Maybe the same happened with Saveer after Ishanvi's death? Maybe he didn't tell me lest I got upset. And . . .

Prisha saw the students getting up and realized that the lecture was over. She was glad. After their break-up even the most random, unrelated thing would lead her into wondering about Saveer. *Nobody talks about how long the postmortem of a relationship takes place within us*, Prisha thought while collecting her belongings. *And what do the findings lead us to? If you are still in love with the person, then the discovery will lead you to believe that a perfect love story was compromised with the break-up. And if you hated the person, then you will conclude that whatever happens, happens for the best.* Prisha knew that it would take a long, lonesome, tedious and an emotionally wrecking postmortem of her relationship with Saveer to get back to being normal.

She joined Gauri outside the classroom.

'Are you going to attend the next lecture?' Gauri asked.

'No. I need to go to office and collect a few things,' Prisha said. 'Aren't you coming?' she asked.

'No. I don't have anything left there. I emailed Krishna my resignation,' Gauri said, tapping furiously on her phone.

I do have a few things there, Prisha thought and said, 'Still, you can come with me.'

'Actually,' Gauri looked up at her, 'Karthik is also free now. We were thinking of having coffee.'

For a moment, something poked Prisha.

'Yeah, sure,' she said, smiling weakly.

'See you later.'

Suddenly, Prisha was all alone. It was clear that Gauri and Karthik were into each other. Diggy was gone. What does that leave me with? A cold nothingness within and outside.

Prisha drove Diggy's scooty to office. She was about to park at the usual spot when she saw some other two-wheeler parked there. Would this happen to what she had cultivated within Saveer as well? Someone will come by sooner or later. Like she had, after Ishanvi's death. Prisha parked her scooty elsewhere and went inside.

There was a girl sitting at her desk. She excused herself and picked up the coffee mug that had Saveer and her picture on it, a few family photographs that she had pinned on the board in front of her desk and some other stuff that she had kept in the drawer. Once she was done, Prisha took a deep breath. Now was the time to do what she had come here for. She went ahead and knocked on Saveer's office before entering.

For a moment, Saveer looked speechless upon seeing her. He couldn't think of anything.

'Relax,' Prisha said. 'I'm not here to ask you to patch up or anything. I respect your decision. I came here to collect my stuff. I have sent Krishna my resignation via email.'

Saveer remained quiet.

'I wanted to thank you. Your decision to break up with me has helped me grow up. I won't say I like this feeling but I'm glad that I encountered it through the person I love. I know few people can say that. So yeah, thanks. Take care,' Prisha said and turned to leave. Then she stopped.

'One more thing.' She walked up to him. Saveer remained seated on his chair. Before he knew what had happened, Prisha had had her last kiss.

'I thought we owed each other that,' she said and immediately left, not waiting for an answer. Once she was out of the room, Saveer wondered when the time would come when he would scoop her up in his arms and tell her that they were in it for life. Sighing, he checked his watch. It was time to go home.

Saveer entered his own house suspiciously. *What if the woman was already there?* Though the camera feed told him that the house was empty, Saveer was alert as he crossed the living room and went to the kitchen first and then to the bedroom. He checked the washroom and the store room, after which he relaxed. The next thing on his mind was what he couldn't decipher from the footage. He went to the wall clock in the living room and checked the time and then glanced at his wrist watch. Both read: 6.50 p.m. Saveer frowned. He immediately scooted to his bedroom. The digital clock on his bedside table showed the same time. He remembered clearly that the woman had picked up the digital clock in her hands. Saveer too picked it up. Something struck him. He kept the digital clock back on the table and sat on the bed with his phone. He googled the exact time. The search result flashed the exact Indian Standard Time: 6.49.37. *One minute and thirty odd seconds ahead.* Was this the change the woman had made to the clock? He wasn't sure but there was something about the time that bothered him. Like it had some strange significance. He started pacing up and down the room, thinking hard. Minutes passed. Then he suddenly muttered, 'Shit!' He remembered exactly why. It was around seven years ago. It had happened three or four times. Ishanvi was particular about everything—almost as if she had OCD, especially regarding time. She was always punctual and hated those who weren't. There were many instances when Saveer had got late in meeting her and she had got angry. She was in the bedroom when she had pointed out to him that his clocks were always a minute and a half ahead. She would diligently wind them back to the right time. It wasn't out of the ordinary back then, but now it seemed significant. Saveer was lost in deep thought when his phone rang. It was Shetty.

'Hello, Mr Rathod. I called to inform you that we have watched the footage meticulously. Unfortunately, the identity of the woman isn't clear. Anyway, we are deploying few plain-clothed policemen around your house to keep a tab. Especially tonight.'

'Great. Thanks for the cooperation, officer,' Saveer said.

'We put on uniforms to serve people. So no thanks, Mr Rathod.' Saveer was all charged up. It's just a matter of time now, he thought. A mystery which had engulfed his entire life and cost him all his dear ones would finally be unravelled once the woman was caught.

Saveer went to the washroom, stripped off his T-shirt and turned his back to the mirror, then craned his neck to read:

I will fuck your every happiness.

'Who are you, damn it!' Saveer yelled.

Since his shirt wasn't close to his mouth, his voice sounded far off through the earphones. But the woman figured out just what he had said.

'Well,' she said, 'I'm Saveer Rathod. It's you who has conveniently forgotten who you are.' She looked deadpan serious in her reflection in a mirror.

22

It was around eleven in the night when a man singing a Kannada song stumbled into the lane where Saveer's house was. While crossing his house, he suddenly collapsed on the ground. He sounded like a drunk. But in reality he wasn't. He was instructed to lie down next to Saveer's house. He was an incognito policeman. As the man collapsed on the ground, he glanced at another man standing at a distant cigarette shop. He was smoking and talking to someone over the phone. He was a cop as well. He, in turn, kept glancing at the window of a house from time to time. The lights were off and the curtains were drawn but there was a team of two men with loaded revolvers, waiting to jump into action if the need arose. Saveer's house was under police supervision as promised by Shetty. All of them were waiting for the woman.

Inside his house, Saveer was restless. He avoided dinner that night. He had seen the woman spike the vegetables and the chicken earlier that day. *Who knows what else had been tampered with.* He had carried a few bottles of Bisleri from office and finished them one at a time while waiting for the woman. He didn't know when he fell asleep. When he woke up in the morning, his first thought was that he had been drugged. Seconds later, he realized that he had fallen asleep on his own. He looked around. Everything seemed normal. He took his phone and called up Shetty.

'Good morning, Mr Rathod.' Shetty sounded as if he his mouth was stuffed with food.

'Good morning, officer. Any leads?'

'Nothing. My men kept waiting. Didn't sleep at all. But nobody came. Don't worry. You keep the camera on when you leave the house. My men will be keeping an eye on visitors.'

'Sure, I'll do that. Thanks.'

Saveer went to office and kept the live feed of his phone on at all times. He kept glancing at it in between work but every time the footage showed an empty house, he felt frustrated.

Nobody came that night. Or on the next two nights. A week passed and nothing happened except Saveer developing a habit of checking his phone's live feed every few minutes. Nine days after the police deployed its men to supervise his house, Shetty called up Saveer.

'Hello, Mr Rathod.'

'Hi, officer,' Saveer said. He was in his office. When his phone flashed Shetty's name, Saveer felt thrilled. He was hoping there was some good news.

'It has been some time and absolutely nothing has happened,' Shetty said instead.

'Yes. I know.' Saveer's hopes were immediately dashed.

'So I had a suggestion.'

'Please, tell me.' *Don't tell me you are taking those policemen off*, he thought.

'I was thinking about whatever you told me about this case. The woman who you think is related to this case has killed, according to you, people who were close to you. And then you told me you have broken up with your girlfriend. Correct?'

'Hmm, that's correct.' Saveer had an idea as to where Shetty was steering the conversation to.

'In that case, do you think it leaves the woman, we have been waiting for, any reason to visit your house?'

Saveer thought for some time before responding. It was something which had not struck him.

'I get your point. So what do you suggest?'

'I suggest you patch up with your girlfriend.' Shetty sounded convinced of what he said.

'We have broken off. I don't think it will be possible.'

'Are you sure?'

'Pretty much.'

'Then there's nothing much that we can do. One man will suffice to keep a watch over your house for a few more days. If nothing happens, then we will need to stop the supervision. Please let us know if you come across anything suspicious.'

'For sure.'

Saveer disconnected the call and stood up. He walked towards the big window in his room and pulled the blinds up. He looked outside. *Officer Shetty had made a valid point*, Saveer thought. *There is indeed no reason why the woman should visit me again, considering she knows Prisha and I have broken up. Even the tattoo hints at the same. 'I will fuck your every happiness'. So if there's no happiness, the woman is out of her job.* Saveer turned around. He couldn't believe that he had missed such a vital point. *The woman will be there if I am happy.* But how could he be happy? Not by sleeping around with random women. He never had any hiccup during his Mean Monster phase because he wasn't really happy back then. He was happy when he felt as if he had made a soulful connect with Prisha. It had become a vicious cycle of sorts: if they didn't catch the woman, Saveer would never be able to patch up with Prisha and give their relationship another chance. But to nab her, he would have to seek true happiness, which lay with Prisha. His only option now was to convince Prisha to give themselves another chance, even if it meant pretending to be together, so that they inched closer to nabbing the woman. Saveer ran his fingers through his hair realizing how messy it sounded. *But what other choice do I have?*

He sauntered to his table, picked up his phone and messaged Shetty: *I'll try to reconnect with Prisha.*

'*Great. Keep me posted,*' was the response.

23

Saveer first decided to send Prisha a message.
Hi, can we talk?

He waited, but the message was not delivered even after office hours. *Has she blocked me or something?* He wondered and called her up.

The number you are trying to reach is switched off, an automated voice responded.

Saveer drove straight to Prisha's apartment. He parked his car and went up. He had to only ring once before the door was opened. It was a young boy.

'Yes?' Karthik asked.

Saveer wasn't expecting a boy. Had Prisha already moved on? he wondered. *She has all the right to,* he thought, before saying, 'I wanted to see Prisha.'

'She isn't here right now,' Karthik said.

Saveer was itching to ask who he was. 'Her number is switched off. I need to meet her,' he said instead.

'You are . . . ?'

That should be my question. 'I'm Saveer. A friend of hers.'

'All right. Prisha's phone will be off till tomorrow. She is in the Art Of Living ashram.'

'Alone?'

'No. Her batch from college is there,' Karthik said. Saveer realized there was no point asking the boy anything else. Somehow he was making him uncomfortable. *Did he move in with Prisha?* Saveer left. He googled the ashram's address, put it on his GPS and then headed in that direction. It was around 10 p.m. when he reached there.

There was an air of tranquillity in the ashram. It was as if the peaceful aura had muted the hustle and bustle of city life. He went inside and inquired about the Cross University team. The ashram superintendent put Saveer in touch with the professor who was in charge of the students. The trip was organized so that the students could enjoy two stress-free days from college.

'I don't think I recognize you,' the professor said.

'I'm Saveer Rathod. I'm here to meet an acquaintance. It's urgent.'

'What's his or her name?'

'Prisha Srivastav.'

'Oh, all right. Let me call her.' The professor went inside while Saveer waited. He felt an unlikely nervousness. Some time later, he heard a voice.

'Here.' It was the professor. He was followed by an unsure-looking Prisha. When the professor had mentioned that someone named Saveer Rathod had come to meet her, she had thought that she had officially lost her mind. But now, when she realized that it was indeed Saveer who was standing in front of her, she felt like laughing. She'd jumped at the opportunity to accompany her batch mates to the Art of Living ashram only because she wanted to get a grip on herself. After the break-up, all that she could think of was the separation. As if there was nothing more left to life than that. As the break-up slowly sank in, Prisha tried to remember the relationship for the wonderful things that she had experienced with Saveer. And that was the only reason why she was in the ashram. Now the man responsible for rescuing her from an emotional crisis, helping her discover herself and changing her for ever was standing right in front of her, challenging the very reason why she was in the ashram. *Life has some shitty sense of humour*, she thought and said, 'Yes, sir, he is an acquaintance.'

'All right,' the professor said and excused himself. There was silence as their eyes met.

'How did you know I'm here?' Prisha asked.

'I went to your flat. A guy told me you were here. Who is he?'

Really? You came here to know who the guy in my flat was? 'I don't know,' Prisha said.

'You can tell me if he is your boyfriend. I won't mind,' Saveer said. He'd carried the face of the boy in his mind till he reached the ashram.

'How will I know which guy you saw? Most probably it was Karthik. And no, he isn't my boyfriend. He is Gauri's boyfriend.'

Saveer relaxed. Now it was time to tell her why he had come to the ashram.

'I need to tell you something.'

'Of course. Otherwise two people who swore not to meet again, don't just meet a few days after such a conversation. What is it, Saveer?'

'We are close to nabbing the woman,' Saveer said.

'We?'

'The police and I.'

'Care to explain, please?'

Saveer told the developments in the case.

'So, the police suggested that you and I play the relationship game again. Only this time, it will be a pretence?'

'Kind of.'

'Are you okay with it?'

'I have a request. Can we do it without asking questions?' Saveer said, knowing well that he didn't have answers to anything right now.

'Sure. I'll need one more day in the ashram,' Prisha said and thought, *I'll come back here after our pretence is over. I'm sure till then my mind would be even more fucked than what it is right now.*

'That's not an issue. All we need to do is meet once or twice outside like we used to.'

'Like we used to?'

'*Almost* . . . like we used to.'

'Almost . . . one of the two saddest words we had discussed once.'

'And then you stay with me for a few nights.' Saveer stuck to the point.

A few more nights with you? Wow! Get ready for a royal mind-fuck, Prisha.

'Until the woman visits,' he said.

'And we catch her.'

'Yes.'

'I'll see you the day after then?'

'See me where?'

'I'll pick you up. We'll go to some cafe first and then to my house.'

'Hmm.'

'Take care,' he said and was about to leave when Prisha stopped him.

'Saveer!'

'Suppose the woman gets caught, comes out clean about those killings. The police arrests her. What about us then?'

Saveer took his time before replying, 'Right now, I don't know.' However, in his eyes there was a flicker of hope.

'I get it. See you the day after,' Prisha said.

Saveer left.

They met at a cafe as planned. Prisha was stiff when he hugged her. *Was that too a pretence?* she wondered. They ordered coffee and kept quiet. It was one of the most awkward dates Prisha had ever been to. After finishing their coffee, they went to his house.

'If you want, you can go to my bedroom and study,' Saveer said. 'I'll make myself comfortable here for the night.' He was ensconced on the couch.

'I know asking questions weren't part of the deal but I have to ask you something,' Prisha said.

'Okay.'

'Did you feel jealous when you saw the boy at my flat the other day?'

'Jealous? Of course, not. Why would a teenager make me jealous?' Saveer said. The way he vehemently denied the possibility made Prisha smile faintly. She knew he had been jealous.

'I think you were,' Prisha said, amused.

'Then probably I was,' Saveer said, without looking at her. The indirect confession made him look undeniably cute. At that moment, Prisha wanted to pull his cheeks, ruffle his hair and kiss him hard.

'Do you mind if I stay here? I need to study but I don't have to be alone in any room to do that.'

'Sure.' They stayed in the living room throughout the night. The dinner was intentionally packed from outside and Saveer dozed off soon after eating his food. Prisha continued to study. But with Saveer lying on the couch, she was getting distracted. So she got herself a stool and sat on it with her back to him. Not that he was looking. Few hours later, when she felt she couldn't last any longer, Prisha closed her books. She stood up and found Saveer softly snoring with his mouth open. Prisha tiptoed towards him and knelt down on the floor. Her mouth was close to his now.

I'm young but no fool, she thought looking at his face. *I know you could have chosen not to take the pain of seeking me and perhaps lived your life the way you used to, being Mean Monster, after Ishanvi's death. But the fact that you are hell-bent on doing so, even going to the extent of facing embarrassment and reaching out to me, tells me that you too have the same thing on your mind, Saveer. We shall be together once this person is caught. And I shall wait till then. Whether it takes a day or an eternity, I will wait for you, Saveer.* Prisha kissed him lightly on his chin and gently closed his mouth. Saveer stirred in his sleep but didn't wake up. Prisha went to the other couch and lay down there. Soon sleep took over.

When Saveer didn't get any call or message from Shetty, he understood that nothing had happened. He went to office while Prisha went back home. This routine continued for over a week. Prisha was happy to comply without any complaints. She was getting used to the silence between them. Deep inside, she knew that the silence was only an attempt to bring back the words. She too wanted to nab the woman who was the reason for their break-up. She didn't tell Gauri that she was staying over at Saveer's place. Gauri too didn't try to find out as it gave her an opportunity to be with Karthik.

On the eleventh night, Saveer said, 'This is the last night. If the woman doesn't visit tonight, I've decided to call the police off. I can't keep asking you to come here every night. It will hamper your studies and . . .'

'And?' Prisha prayed desperately for the woman to turn up.

'And this is not how things can run.'

'Then how should things run?'

'The way they were. Before you came into my life,' Saveer said. Prisha didn't say anything after that. The following morning, she went back to her flat. The woman had not turned up. Saveer went to office and called up Shetty.

'Good morning, officer. I think I'm done with this. Please feel free to call off your men.'

'Are you sure, Mr Rathod?'

'I am. I don't have the right to waste everyone's time on the basis of a hunch. I'll pull out the cameras as well.'

'As you say. But let me know if you ever need any help.'

'I sure will. Thank you so much, officer.' Saveer cut the call. He felt frustrated, not so much because the woman had not come back again but because he couldn't accept that Prisha and he couldn't live a life together. He left work on time, went home instead of the gym, had an early dinner and slept off, like he used to when he was drugged. Next morning, he woke up with a headache. Saveer still couldn't guess that his food was freshly spiked. He realized that he had forgotten to pull out the secret cameras. He switched on his phone to de-link it when he jumped from his seat. He saw the woman again in the feed. She had visited him last night. The time showed 2 a.m. She left at 4.35 a.m. Saveer wanted to throw the phone away in anger. But he somehow managed to maintain his cool and went for a shower. In office, Saveer couldn't wrap his head around the coincidence. Why did she visit him the same day that he called off the supervision? The only other possibility was that she knew what Saveer was up to. *But how?* He kept an eye on his phone's live feed while working. Some time in the afternoon, he noticed that the woman came back again. He was at *Ishanvi's*, having lunch alone. At night, the woman had simply been sitting beside the bed, on the rocking chair, but right now she was going through his wardrobe.

'What's she doing?' Saveer mumbled. The moment he uttered the words, he saw the woman pressing her right hand against her ears. Saveer frowned.

'Hi, how are you?' Saveer said to nobody in particular. He wanted to check the woman's reaction. The woman kept pressing her hand against her ear.

'I forgot to pull out the cameras,' Saveer said with his eyes on the screen. The woman stood still for some time and then rushed out of the house.

Damn! She can hear me, Saveer thought. *That explains the coincidence. But how can she?*

Saveer rushed back to his office. He went to the washroom attached to his cabin. He kept his phone on the wash basin and frisked himself. He found nothing.

There has to be something, he kept telling himself. He took off his shirt and started checking it fastidiously. Till he got to the cufflink. He inspected it closely. And then, he smirked.

Caught you, bitch!

24

Saveer wore back his shirt. He still couldn't come to terms with the fact that someone had planted a microphone in his cufflink. What could have motivated the woman to go to *this* extent to keep tabs on his daily activities? And that too for twenty-five years? *Ok, maybe not twenty-five years of putting microphones on my cufflinks*, he thought, but if this woman was really involved in all the killings, what was the trigger? Saveer told Krishna he was leaving for a meeting. He was extra careful in choosing his words. When you know you have been bugged, you tend to become overtly cautious.

Saveer drove to the nearest mall, mindful of being followed. He parked the car and went inside. Spotting a men's apparel store, he walked in and selected a few T-shirts. He changed into one of them in the trial room and left with the rest and his old shirt in a shopping bag. As he drove out of the parking lot, he thought of calling up Shetty but immediately rejected the idea. *What if his phone was also tapped?* Saveer drove straight to the police station.

He waited for some time for the sub-inspector to arrive.

'Sir is out of station for two days for some official work,' the sub-inspector informed him. 'Anything you wish to be conveyed?'

My phone might be tapped, but certainly not his, Saveer thought and said, 'If you could please connect me to him over the phone, it would be great.'

'Certainly,' the sub-inspector said and dialled the officer's number on his mobile phone.

'Hello, sir, there is one Mr Rathod with me who wants to talk to you . . . Certainly, sir.' He handed over the phone to Saveer.

'Hello, officer. It's me, Saveer Rathod.'

'Mr Rathod, have you lost my number?' Shetty asked.

'No, I have it. Just that I have stumbled upon something,' Saveer said and then went on to tell him how he had discovered that he had been bugged all this while. That was how the woman had managed to evade them.

'In that case, I don't think it would be that difficult to catch her, unless she decides not to visit at all. I shall order a search around your place as well. I'm coming back after a few days. Let's meet once I'm back.'

'Sure, officer. I'll wait for you.'

'Till then could you do me a favour, Mr Rathod?'

'Anything, officer.'

'I shall ask the forensic expert to get in touch with you. This is the same person who wrote the forensic report on Digambar Sethia. He had called me some time ago to inform that whether a rape had happened or not could not be conclusively said. Digambar's anal muscles were indeed ruptured but there were no marks, no semen or anything which could suggest that it was a definite sexual attack.'

Saveer listened intently.

'What does the forensic person have to do with me?' he asked.

'He will take your blood sample for a test. That's all,' Shetty said matter-of-factly.

'What am I missing, officer?'

'It's a policeman's hunch. A policeman who has spent nineteen years dealing with crime and criminals.'

'I never doubted your credentials, officer.'

'I didn't say you did, Mr Rathod. All that I am saying is that I have a hunch.'

'What is your hunch?' Saveer asked.

'That the woman is related to you.'

Saveer took some time before replying, 'All right. I shall wait for the forensic person.'

'Thank you, Mr Rathod. I cannot be sure but that's how we crack cases. We rely on our suspicions, hunches and sort out possibilities from multiple theories, one at a time, till we arrive at a conclusion. And one single killer.'

'I understand.'

Saveer disconnected the call and left the police station. Shetty's words kept ringing in his ears throughout his drive back home. *The woman could be related to you.* But all his family members were dead. Saveer continued driving with a clogged mind.

* * *

Prisha was finishing one of her assignments at home. Since Diggy's death, Gauri had shifted to his room. They were looking for a third flatmate to make the rent affordable but had had no luck so far. The other reason for Gauri to shift into Diggy's room was Karthik. She had become serious with him though she hadn't told Prisha anything about it. Not that Prisha had asked.

Prisha heard the main door unlock. Half a minute later, Gauri peeped inside her room.

'Got a minute?'

'Hey, sure. What's up?' Prisha closed her laptop and sat up on her bed.

'Nothing much. Just that we haven't caught up lately.'

'Yeah, I know.' Prisha knew it could be an awkward discussion.

'I wanted to thank you, Prisha.'

'Thank me?'

'For telling me those things you did when Karthik was approaching me and I, like a dumbo, was neglecting him. I thought about what you said and realized I couldn't possibly let go of someone who is meant for me, for someone who never was.'

Prisha smiled.

'I'm happy that it is going smoothly with Karthik.'

'He is a little slow at grasping things but otherwise he is a gem of a person.'

'That's what matters, right? I think we girls get it wrong most of the time. It's not about how our partner treats us but how the partner makes us believe what we deserve each and every day. Sanjeev made you believe that you deserved to be the other woman in his life with his clever manipulation of words. Utkarsh made me believe that I deserved nobody. Whereas Saveer made me realize that I deserved a healthy relationship sans betrayal,' Prisha said. She thought she said a little too much.

'I totally get it,' Gauri said. 'Have Saveer and you really broken off?' There was guilt in her voice for pushing Prisha and Saveer into calling it quits.

'Yes. We have. But will you call me a fool if I tell you we are still not done yet?'

Gauri hugged her. 'I'll pray that you guys aren't done yet,' she whispered into her ears.

Prisha's phone rang. Gauri broke the hug and went to her room. It was Prisha's mother. She took the call. While listening to her updates of the day, Prisha kept thinking if Saveer and she would ever get back together. And then she suddenly interrupted her mother with a question.

'Were you ever in love with someone before you married Papa?'

'What?' Her mother thought that she had heard her daughter wrong. Prisha repeated her question.

'What kind of a question is this?'

'Mumma, it is a simple question. I'm not Ayushee. I'm a grown up girl. You can tell me.'

'Are you out of your mind?'

'I don't understand parents. First, they want their kids to be honest with them and when they ask them questions, hoping that they would give them frank answers, they pretend it's not a worthy enough question.'

'But . . .'

'Mumma, please. It's important.'

The urgency in Prisha's voice made her mother realize that her daughter had indeed grown up. She could talk to her like a friend. Truth be told, Mrs Srivastav had been waiting for the day her little girl would grow up to be her friend. Someone, who wouldn't judge her but rather learn from her experiences. Someone, to whom she could open those windows of her long ago feelings.

'There was this guy in my locality. But I was never in a relationship with him.'

'And?'

'And? Nothing more. I got married early. He was still studying. And your father was settled, had a job.'

Prisha could sense an unsaid pain in her mother's voice.

'Do you miss him, Mumma?'

'I love your father. I love you and Ayushee.'

'That's not the answer to my question.'

'I have never been with him. So I was always used to his absence. You miss someone if you have had him by your side,' her mother said.

The two women took a pause, and then changed the topic. They had now understood each other's past and present. Mrs Srivastav understood that her daughter must have gone through a genuine heartbreak. But she also knew that she would engulf the pain like an ocean engulfs a whole mass of land without letting anyone see any trace of it. She had, after all, her blood. Prisha, on the other hand, knew she had gained a friend in her mother that day. She was right. And she was lucky not to have enjoyed the guy's presence. Else it would have been difficult for her. Like it was difficult for Prisha because she had known Saveer's presence. It would be a lifelong difficulty. Unsurmountable. Every relationship leaves behind either an ocean or a desert. But Saveer had left her with an emotional mountain. She would never be able to scale it and see what lay on the other side. It would either be this or nothing else. No one else.

Saveer reached home. He had a weight on his heart. Maybe a hot shower would help, he thought. It didn't. Shetty's words that the woman could be related to him, kept playing on his mind on a loop. He brought out all his shirts from the wardrobe and dumped them on the ground. He would ask someone to first remove and then throw all the cufflinks and take the shirts away. He had started wearing shirts because Ishanvi loved him in tees. She would tell him that he exuded a boyish charm when he wore T-shirts. After she was gone, he couldn't see himself in a T-shirt any more. As he took out the last shirt from the wardrobe, he noticed the small bag where he kept all his important documents. It had been some time since he had opened that bag.

Saveer took out the bag and sat in the rocking chair. He pulled out the documents—original mark sheets of Class X and XII, pass certificates, graduation and post-graduation certificates, some pay slips, his first offer letter and . . . he stopped at his birth certificate. He pulled out the certificate and casually looked it over. His name was mentioned: Saveer Rathod. The name of the nursing home where he was born was mentioned: Jamuna Das Nursing Home, Udaipur. The date was 9 November 1982. And the time was 09.10.01. Saveer kept staring at the time. There was something about it which disturbed him. He took a picture of the birth certificate on his phone and stuffed it back in the bag. There were a few other documents. He went through each one of them—bank papers, company deed and . . . an old paper. It was his computer-generated kundali. An instant smile came his lips. His mother had got it from an astrologer. All the memories of his mother came rushing back to him. He was almost revelling in them with a nostalgic smile when he noticed the time of his birth mentioned in the kundali as 09.11.38. On top of the kundali, was his name. Saveer frowned. He took out his birth certificate once again. He matched the times. They were different. And the difference was exactly of one minute and thirty-seven seconds.

But then which mother would goof up her child's birth time like that? Saveer wondered.

The woman who had visited him had tampered the clocks with exactly this time difference—one minute and thirty-seven seconds.

25

Saveer couldn't sleep that night. His thoughts led him to a dead end. And everything about the entire episode was absolutely absurd.

The woman is related to you.

For that, she'll have to be a ghost, because none of my family members are alive, Saveer thought as he showered in the morning. The only person who could be alive was his uncle. But he had serious doubts about that. The forensic expert rang the doorbell as he was ordering his breakfast from *Ishanvi's.* He took his blood sample.

'What exactly are you going to do with this?' Saveer asked as he was preparing to leave.

'I'd got some blood sample on Digambar's nails. It wasn't his. There was definitely a scuffle. His anal sphincters were damaged. And there were some other bruises. But his nails had the blood sample of another person. Shetty sir asked me to collect your blood sample as well.'

'What will we arrive at then?'

'If the person whom Digambar had a scuffle with is related to you. If you two have the same bloodline.'

'Hmm, thanks.'

The man was about to leave when Saveer stopped him again.

'How exactly did Digambar die?'

'Lack of oxygen to his brain. My guess is he was smothered to death.'

Of course, the person isn't of my bloodline, Saveer thought as the man left and he settled down on his couch, frowning. But what if the test is positive? *What would I do then?* Everything, from Ishanvi to his birth certificate to his past memories of everyone in his family to Prisha, started playing on his mind. He held his head in his hands in distress and was about to lie down when he heard his phone ringing in the bedroom.

It was his assistant.

'Yeah, Krishna.'

'Sir, just wanted to inform you that the meeting with the Dubai-based sponsors scheduled for today has been postponed to tomorrow.'

'Okay.'

Saveer cut the call. A few seconds later, he called back Krishna.

'Krishna, please push the sponsor meeting to day after tomorrow. And arrange for the phone number of Jamuna Das Nursing Home in Udaipur.'

'Sure, sir.' Saveer wanted to check the authenticity of the birth certificate. It was a premonition—he felt something major could be hidden in the time difference. *One minute and thirty-seven seconds*, he murmured. Krishna called him after half an hour. He gave him the landline number of the nursing home in Udaipur. Saveer noted it down and immediately called up.

'Hello,' a middle-aged man, sounding a tad bit cross, answered.

'Is this Jamuna Das Nursing Home?' Saveer asked.

'Yes. How may I help you?'

'I was born in the nursing home years ago. I wanted to ask a few questions,' Saveer said and instantly realized that he had put across the query suspiciously.

'Are you a policeman or someone?' The man sounded worried.

'No. I was born in Jamuna Das Nursing Home.'

'When?'

'9 November 1982.'

'So?' The man sounded clueless.

'I wanted some information regarding my birth certificate.'

'*Achha, achha.*' The man sounded as if he had understood whatever Saveer was talking about. 'Come to the nursing home. We'll see what we can do for you.'

'I can ask this over the phone also.'

'But I can't answer this over the phone. You come here and then we'll see what we can do,' the man repeated.

Saveer understood that he would not find out anything unless he bribed him. But for that he would have to visit Udaipur. He thought for a few minutes before calling up Krishna again.

'Yes, sir.'

'Krishna, please book a round trip for me to Udaipur. Push all meetings for day after tomorrow.'

'Right, sir. When do you want to leave?'

'Today, at the earliest,' Saveer said.

'Sure, sir.'

Saveer opened the photo gallery of his phone and tapped on the picture of his birth certificate. He zoomed in and kept staring at the time.

* * *

In the house next door, the woman kept her ear piece down on the dressing table. She had tested it several times. Her microphones were working fine until last evening when she could no longer hear any of Saveer's conversations. She knew it could mean only one thing— that her microphones in the cufflinks and some of the buttons had been discovered.

She went to the mirror and while looking at her reflection switched on the hair dryer. *It took you so many years to even sniff my presence*, she thought while drying her hair, *and now you want to find me so fast. I only hope you are ready for what it may trigger.* She switched off the dryer.

She'd heard something. Hurrying to the window, she parted the curtain a little and noticed an Ola cab waiting in front of Saveer's house. Seconds later, Saveer came out, and got into the cab. The woman frowned. *He never takes cabs*, she thought. The woman wore her favourite printed floral dress, matching pumps and pearl earrings and a pearl necklace. She chose a deep red lipstick. She left after wearing a pair of big dark shades. She worked as an office supervisor in one of the outlets of Red Dart Courier Service. Close to her office, she stopped a man on the road and asked, 'Excuse me, I forgot my phone back home. I need to make an urgent call.'

'Yeah, sure,' the man said and gave his phone to her. She thanked him and dialled a landline number. She moved a few paces in front so that the man couldn't hear her. 'Hi, I'm talking from St Teresa High School. I wanted to talk to Mr Saveer Rathod. This is regarding a project involving the girls of our school,' she said over the phone.

'Sir is out of station from today.'

'Till?'

'Day after, but that day is full. Could you please call on Thursday? I shall fix up a meeting,' Krishna said.

'Sure. Where is he travelling to?' she asked, and then realized it sounded intrusive. 'Actually we have representatives in a lot of places so just in case . . .' she quickly added.

'He is flying to Udaipur for personal reasons. He won't be free for business till he is back. What did you tell your name was, ma'am?'

The mere mention of Udaipur made her heart skip a beat. She knew what he was heading for.

'Hello?' Krishna said, but the woman cut the call and gave the phone back to the man on the street.

'Thanks,' she said and walked to her office.

* * *

The flight to Udaipur was on time. He didn't have any luggage. He had booked a room at Radisson Blu but when he got into the cab sent by the hotel, he asked the driver to take him to Jamuna Das Nursing Home. The driver told him it was in Sadarpura. Though he was born in Udaipur, Saveer hadn't really lived there for a long time. His only memory of that place was playing in the lane where he used to live with his parents and brother. His father had set up his business in Jaipur and later in Delhi so they shifted early. He looked at his watch. There was a sense of restlessness in him. Saveer took a deep breath to calm his nerves.

* * *

Her job profile was simple. She had to cater to customers, accept their couriers, give them the receipts after accepting the payments and later hand the packages over to the pick-up guy. The office was a small space on MG Road. Except for the guard outside, she was the only one working in the office for the last four years. But six months ago, another man had joined her, dividing her workload. And increasing her problems. Sarthak, a middle-aged, married man, would relentlessly lech at her. She was the most gorgeous woman he had ever seen in his life. The woman knew about his intentions but didn't want to make any noise till he crossed a line. Every now and then, he would find a reason to come close to her. Sometimes, he would deliberately drop the stapler and while picking it up, brush his hands against her body; or at times it would be the office landline on which if he got any call he would deliberately stand close to her and talk. Making her uncomfortable gave him a kick.

The guard had gone for a quick smoke when she entered the office. Sarthak smiled at her. She didn't. She had just sat down when Sarthak approached her and suddenly grabbed hold of her hand.

'I know you like this,' he said. The woman looked at his hand and then at him. She had a problem with men. Especially when they touched her. If she was allowed, she would have killed all the men in this world at one go. She removed his hand. He was surprised by her strength. But his lecherous smile was back when he heard her say, 'Come inside the store.'

The woman stood up and walked into the store room, which was a small space behind the front office and beside the washroom. Sarthak immediately had a hard on. This was the moment he had been jerking off to for a long time. He stood up and followed her inside. The moment he entered, he felt someone push him roughly. Sarthak stumbled towards the wall. The woman grabbed his neck, pinning him against the wall, and with her other hand, she held his balls in a vice-like grip. She glared at him and said, 'I've tolerated you ever since you joined. But let me tell you, I'll be in a very bad mood from now on. If you touch me again, even if it is accidentally,' she gripped his balls harder, 'I will squash these sorry nuts with my bare hands.' She released him and went out. Sarthak's heart was in his mouth. His balls were aching. It took him a couple of minutes to register what had just happened.

* * *

Saveer's cab stopped right outside Jamuna Das Nursing Home. He had no memory of the place. It looked like the small building had been recently painted. The hospital was buzzing with activity. Saveer made his way to the small reception counter, where a man was sitting.

'Hi, I'm Saveer Rathod and I needed some information about my birth certificate.'

The man looked up at him. He squinted his eyes for a moment and then his face cracked into a smile.

'You are the one who called me this morning?' he asked.

'Yes.'

'So, what can I do for you?'

After giving him a Rs 2000 note, the man took Saveer to a room upstairs where all their documents were kept inside an old steel almirah. Amid cobwebs and covered with a thick blanket of dust was a huge heap of files. The man dusted as much as he could and while coughing found a file which was marked 1982. Saveer waited anxiously. His request was straight and simple—he just wanted to see their copy of his birth certificate. Especially the time on it. He didn't know what the answer could be but . . . *I'll see after I check the certificate*, he told himself.

After a thorough search, the man found Saveer's birth certificate. He took it out from among a bunch of other documents and gave it to him. There was another certificate along with it. Saveer tried to give it back to the man when he realized that the two certificates were stapled together. He read the one above. The name on it said Saveer Rathod. The date and time: 9 November, 09.10.01. The second certificate was that of Veer Rathod's. The date and time read: 9 November, 09.11.38. Saveer frowned. He never knew his brother was his twin. And also that he was the elder one. His parents had always told him that he was the younger one. But the certificate clearly stated that Veer was the younger one.

'Sir, can we leave now? I've other things to do as well,' the man said.

'Yes. Thank you for this,' Saveer said. He photographed both the certificates, handed him another Rs 500 and left the nursing home.

On the way to the hotel, Saveer felt his head reeling. How could he have not known that his brother was his twin? Why was he told that he was the younger one? Saveer ran his fingers through his hair, feeling nervous. Why would he be fed lies about his own brother? Saveer simply didn't know what to think about. The only person possibly alive in his family was his uncle. Raghu uncle. But the last time he'd met him was with his mother. They had gone to Vaishno Devi a year after his father's death and had accidentally ran into him. His disciples had brought him there for blessings as he was still paralysed. Raghu uncle, however, failed to recognize his sister-in-law and his nephew. And right now, Saveer didn't even know if he was still alive or, if so, where he could be. Had he been in touch, he could've thrown some light on the problem. But reaching his uncle was a dead end as well.

* * *

The woman left her office on time. She'd been thinking about Saveer's move, sipping coffee in a cafe on MG Road. She paid the bill and left. She walked till the metro station. She approached a man walking out of the station and borrowed his phone, citing the same excuse as before. She called up Saveer's number. A moment later, the phone was picked up.

'Hello?' Saveer said. It was the first time that the woman had directly talked to him.

'Hello?' he said again.

'Hello, Mr Smarty Pants. You have come a little too close to me for your own good. Now, I'll have to do something so you keep your distance.'

'Who is this?' Saveer sounded tensed.

'Sshhh, just listen. From now onwards, Prisha will stay with me. Don't worry, I'll keep her alive. You will see her a few months from now. On your thirty-sixth birthday to be precise. But she won't talk to you then. She won't hear you. She won't even see you. Do I need to tell you why? Because I'll kill her on your thirty-sixth birthday.'

Before Saveer could utter another word, the woman had cut the call.

26

Terrified, Saveer called back the number. After a few rings, a man picked up the phone.

'Who was the woman who spoke to me right now?' Saveer asked. There was an urgency in his voice.

'She just walked inside the metro station.'

'Who are you?' Saveer asked.

'I'm Ranjan. Who are you?'

'Could you please call her?' Saveer almost pleaded.

'She just entered the metro station. And I've to rush home. I'm sorry.' He cut the line.

'Fuck shit!' Saveer threw the phone on the bed. He knew talking to the man was useless. He was so close to unmasking the woman. In the last twenty-five years, not once had the woman approached him, but now she had. The call had proved that she was involved in all the killings, including Diggy's. But Prisha's life was in danger. He immediately called her up. Unfortunately, the call didn't get through.

Where the hell are you, Prisha! he muttered under his breath and dialled again. This time an automated voice said, 'The number you are trying to reach is unavailable.'

Since he didn't have Gauri's number, Saveer instead texted: *Call the moment you read this.* He sent it to Prisha. He was scheduled to fly back the next morning. He called up Krishna to check if an earlier flight back to Bengaluru was available. Krishna took ten minutes to revert, only to say there was none. Saveer knew he was losing his grip on things. He took a few deep breaths and told himself that he couldn't do anything now. Except pray that the woman didn't get to Prisha before he reached her. His phone rang. It was Shetty. As he stared at the name, he had a gut feeling that it was bad news. He picked up the call.

'Yes, officer,' Saveer said.

'Thanks for all your cooperation, Mr Rathod. I got the medical report.'

Saveer had a sinking feeling as he heard Shetty say, 'My hunch was right. The person who attacked Digambar is indeed related to you. It is the same bloodline.'

There was no response from Saveer.

'I'm back in Bengaluru,' the officer continued, 'It would be great if you could come see me immediately. Mr Rathod? Hello?'

Saveer went cold.

'Mr Rathod, you there?'

'Yes . . . Yes, officer. I'm actually in Udaipur for some work. Let me come meet you tomorrow when I reach Bengaluru,' he managed to mumble.

'Great.'

'I received a phone call from the woman who had broken into my house.'

'What? When?'

'Few minutes before you called.'

'What did she say?'

'Prisha's life is in danger.' Saveer could feel himself breaking down while uttering the words. 'I tried calling her but her phone is out of reach.'

'Don't worry. Just text me her address. I'll send my men immediately. She will be safe. Just don't worry. Also, send me the number from which the woman had called up.' Shetty cut the call.

With trembling hands, Saveer typed out Prisha's address and the phone number from which he had got the call and sent it to Shetty. He sat down on the bed with a thud. He'd never felt so weak before. First, the birth certificate confusion, then finding out for the first time in his life about his twin brother, and now, that this woman was related to him. Could all these pieces be put together to get the real story that had remained a mystery so far? But before all that, Prisha had to be warned. Her life was in danger. Saveer checked his phone. The message was yet to be delivered to her.

* * *

Prisha was in two minds. Whether to plunge her hand into the water and pull out the phone or let it be. She was in one of the ladies' washrooms at Forum Mall. She had been peeing while talking to her mother. When she had stood up to flush, the phone balanced precariously between her ear and her shoulder had slipped into the commode. Prisha wanted to retrieve it but couldn't bring herself to plunging her hand into the water and pulling the phone out. She thought of calling the housekeeping staff. She went out. Gauri and Karthik were standing outside, talking. She spotted a housekeeping staffer standing nearby. Prisha approached the woman and took her to the washroom only to realize that some other girl had flushed the toilet. The phone was gone. Irritated, she went out. She told Gauri and Karthik what had happened. They were supposed to catch a movie together and had been in the mall since early evening.

'It's okay. You guys go. I'll just make a call to Mumma,' Prisha said, taking Gauri's phone. *Better explain the situation before she begins to panic,* she thought. After promising to buy another phone the first thing next morning, Prisha hung up.

'I'll push off. Need to complete an assignment. You guys carry on with the movie,' she said, handing the phone back to Gauri.

Prisha asked the cab driver to drop her off at a garden close to her apartment. She wanted to sit in the open, alone, for some time before going inside. Prisha sat on one of the empty benches in a corner of the garden. In the distance a few boys were playing football. It was the same bench on which Diggy and she were sitting on the night they were attacked by the hooligans. A lot had happened since then. Diggy was no more, Gauri was busy with Karthik, and she was back to being single. Like she was on that night. She wondered what Saveer must be up to at that moment. She would feel a strong urge to reconnect with him at times, but would hold herself back. There was no point unless . . . Prisha's train of thoughts was interrupted by a woman who came and sat beside her.

'Pretty lonely here,' she said. Prisha glanced at her.

'Yeah,' she responded.

'I like it this way. Few humans, more peace. What say?'

Prisha noticed that the woman wasn't looking at her while talking. Her hair fell on her face in such a way that she couldn't see her properly. Her voice was not exactly sweet, but it had a certain warmth.

'I love people. It's good to be with the one you love,' Prisha said.

'I hate people. And I hate love,' the woman replied almost instantly. There was a hint of hostility in her voice, which Prisha found inexplicable.

'I hope you understand the meaning of Complete Love one day. Then you would stop hating it.'

'I have understood the meaning of complete hatred. Does that help?'

Prisha felt weird sitting and talking to a stranger who sounded like a wacko. She decided to leave. When she was about to stand up, she felt the woman's hand on her shoulder.

'There's something on your forehead,' she said, making Prisha sit down. Just as Prisha tried to feel what it was, the woman punched her on her temples. A phoenix-eye fist punch. The next moment Prisha had collapsed on the bench, unconscious.

As usual, neat! the woman whispered to herself.

Saveer woke up with a start in his hotel room in Udaipur. He didn't remember it but the aftertaste told him it had been his worst nightmare ever. He checked his phone. It was 10.30 p.m. Only three hours had passed since he had called up Shetty. He didn't know when exactly he had dozed off. Saveer checked the message he had sent to Prisha. It was still undelivered. He was about to call her up when his phone flashed Shetty's name. He picked it up.

'Mr Rathod, we are sorry. We couldn't locate Prisha at her address. And her roommate, miss Gauri, says she had lost her phone earlier in a mall's washroom in the evening. As of now she is untraceable but my men are on it. I'm sure . . .'

Saveer didn't even hear the rest of the sentence. He had broken into a cold sweat knowing that his nightmare had perhaps turned real somewhere.

27

It was excruciating pain which woke up Prisha. She didn't know where she was, what time it was, or what had happened after the woman had punched her. She was only aware of an acute pain in her knee joints and in her elbows. As she slowly opened her eyes, she realized she was lying sideways, with her hands and legs tied up and her mouth gagged.

'I had to bundle you into a bag to get you here. The joints may hurt for a couple of days. Though I've given you an injection to dull the pain,' the woman said. She was sitting across from her. Prisha tried to say something.

'I can pull it out if you promise not to scream. Not that anybody will hear you anyway.' There was a pan on an induction cooktop. The woman was boiling tea. She turned around and put a little sugar in the pan and with her back to Prisha, said, 'Just that I don't like noise. Especially screams. Helpless screams.'

Prisha nodded when the woman turned around. She pulled out the cloth from Prisha's mouth. She couldn't see the woman's face clearly. She was wearing big shades and had thick, long hair. *Was she the same woman Diggy was mad about?*

'Where . . . Where am I?' Prisha asked. The woman helped her sit up. Once Prisha was comfortable, the woman went back to the pan.

'All you need to know is that you are somewhere safe,' she said. Prisha looked around. It looked like the interior of a house boat with a corrugated bamboo roof and bamboo walls.

There was water at one end, land on the other. They were harboured. And it was quiet. As if there was nobody around for miles.

'I discovered this place a year ago,' the woman said, following her eyes. She strained the tea into two paper cups. 'Then I bought this from a fisherman.' She approached Prisha and untied her hands. Prisha felt as if there was no life left in them. She twisted her wrists and stretched her arms a bit before taking one of the cups. The woman sat facing her with the other cup. Prisha could now see her face clearly. It was the same face that she had seen in the mall during the flash mob. The woman read her mind. She removed the shades. Suddenly, Prisha's hands started shaking.

She was strikingly similar to Saveer. 'Who are you?' she asked.

The woman smirked. 'That's the question I've been asking myself for three decades now. *Who am I!* The day I get the answer, I think I'll have a shot at life.'

The woman was glaring at Prisha. She distinguished an indomitable fierceness on her face. As if nothing could touch her. It scared her.

* * *

Saveer had never experienced the kind of anxiety that he had since Shetty had called him up. His message to Prisha was yet to be delivered. He took the scheduled morning flight to Bengaluru and directly headed to the police station from the airport. Shetty was already there. So were Gauri and Karthik. Saveer wasted no time in telling him his actual reason for visiting Udaipur: the fact that he never knew he had a twin brother.

'The case clears up. Well, almost,' Shetty said. 'I'm dead sure the woman is an alias. He is your twin brother.'

'But my brother died twenty-five years ago,' Saveer tried to sound as confident as possible.

'Any death certificate? Any proof? Anything you remember?' the officer asked. Saveer, however, was lost in thoughts. Shetty passed a glass of water towards him. He gulped down some of it. Gauri was sitting across from him. She had uncannily predicted the current situation angrily a day after Diggy's death. Saveer turned away his face from her and racked his brains trying to remember any other detail of his brother but he couldn't. His parents had told him that his uncle had taken Veer to his ashram when he was around five or six. Then he had run away from there and later, he was informed about his death.

'Nothing,' Saveer said. 'I remember nothing concrete to prove to you or to myself that he is dead. And the people who could have are dead.' *Or not reachable*, Saveer thought about his uncle.

'Perhaps, killed,' Shetty said. Saveer remained quiet.

'We have begun a massive manhunt for your brother. Now that we know he is your twin, we also know what he looks like,' Shetty said, leaning back on his chair.

'But it was a woman on the phone,' Saveer said.

'Changing one's voice is no big deal, really.'

After a pause, Saveer added, 'I hope the search is an incognito one because . . .'

'I know he told you he would keep Prisha alive till your birthday. That's a lot of time for us to find him.'

'Alive,' Saveer's voice sounded brittle as he said it.

'Of course!'

Saveer looked at Shetty and then furtively at Gauri.

* * *

A day went by. Prisha didn't know when she had fallen asleep. But when she woke up with her head feeling heavy, She understood that her food was spiked. The body pain had somewhat dulled. She looked around. It was night-time. Everything was bathed in moonlight.

The woman was sitting outside at the edge of the boat, her legs dipped in the water. She was holding a fishing rod.

'Fishing is what I like doing the most. It's such a true reflection of life. To first trick someone using a bait, then catch them, take them out from where they ought to be and then put them where they'll perish. That's the underlying philosophy of this world.' After a pause, she added, 'Of course, I let my fishes back into the water. Unlike life. Unlike people.'

'Were you the one who lured Diggy?' Prisha asked.

'Yes.'

'Why did you rape him?'

The woman looked up at the sky and said, 'I didn't rape him. He touched me inappropriately.'

'Inappropriately?'

'It wasn't his mistake. He was in love with me. And he touched me. He wasn't wrong. But I hate a man's touch. It triggers the beast in me. The same happened that night as well. Before I could calm down, Diggy was no more. He was a nice boy. I'm sorry he had to die. In fact, I am sorry about the other few innocent people who had to die as well.'

Prisha gulped nervously. The last line had come out rather flatly. As if, for her, killing someone was like squashing a mosquito.

After an hour of silence, Prisha asked, 'Was it you who had come to see me at the hospital? Your voice was different.' She knew the answer and yet she wanted to confirm.

The woman smirked, 'Yes, it was me. I had warned you. You can't complain now.'

'Why did you tell me Saveer was not worth it? That I should choose a better person in my next life?' she asked. She saw her roll up a fish. After holding it in her hand for some time, staring at it struggling, the woman threw it back into the water.

'I told you so because it's the truth. He isn't trustworthy.' The woman threw the rod with the bait back in the water.

'Why would you say that? He has never broken my trust.'

'If he hasn't, he will. He broke mine.'

'How? I want to know.' Prisha sounded desperate. There was no response.

'Come on, tell me. Talk to me. You look so much like him. How come? You can't just keep me in the dark,' Prisha insisted. The woman looked at her diabolically. She didn't say anything. Some time later, when the woman went inside the boat, Prisha asked, 'May I know your name at least?'

'You already know my name,' she said. Prisha shook her head. 'It's Saveer Rathod.' She readied her bed beside Prisha and lay down it. Prisha felt nauseated. More so because she knew the woman wasn't kidding. Her only relief was that the drug was taking over her senses. She soon fell asleep.

* * *

Three more days passed. Shetty's team was finally able to locate the house that Saveer's brother had been staying in. They were flummoxed to know that the rent agreement was done in Saveer's name. Neither Saveer nor Shetty could guess why he'd done that. It didn't take the police long to find out where he worked. But there too he had carried on his alias of a woman so convincingly that both her office colleague and the guard were shocked after knowing the truth. When interrogated, the colleague wasn't of much help but the guard told the police that he had mentioned once that he'd go fishing during holidays.

'Fishing?' It made Shetty think of all possibilities.

'Mandya has fishing camps,' Shetty's subordinate said. Mandya, around 100 km from Bengaluru, was where the woman had taken Prisha and held her captive in a boat by a lonely riverside.

28

Nine days had passed since Prisha's disappearance. The police were close, yet far. By now, it wasn't just Saveer and Gauri who were extremely worried but Prisha's parents as well. Her father's blood pressure had shot up. It had not taken them long to understand that their daughter was in danger. When she did not call back a day after telling her mother that she had dropped her phone in the mall's washroom commode, they got suspicious. One call to Gauri and they got to know everything. Prisha had not told them about Diggy's death, and when her father met Saveer after rushing to Bengaluru, he realized that the entire professor-meeting episode was a fake show. Livid and worried, her father warned Saveer of consequences if anything was to happen to his daughter. Saveer said nothing, knowing that he was at fault. *I shouldn't have got involved with Prisha after she was discharged from the hospital*, he thought, regretting. But it was too late to wonder about such things now. The foremost priority for him, for the police, for Gauri and for Prisha's parents was to find her and bring her back alive. Saveer could live with the unsolved mystery surrounding his brother but wouldn't be able to live if Prisha had to pay the price for his mistake.

Back in the boat, during those nine days, Prisha had grown a little used to the woman. She'd said her name was Saveer. But nothing other than that. There were no clarifications. She was still a captive, but somehow, Prisha wasn't scared any more. The monotony of the captivity had made her come to terms with her fear. Her food was still spiked so she slept more than she was awake. And in a way she was happy to sleep away those days. The woman would disappear for some time during the mornings and would be back with food later. She would carry Prisha out and allow her privacy while she finished her ablutions, but her eyes would be blindfolded so she would never know where she was.

But as fear dissipated, impatience started growing inside Prisha. She was tired of the silence, of her restricted life and of the questions that were never answered. On the morning of the tenth day, Prisha lost her cool and started screaming at the woman, demanding to know her plan.

'What is it that you want? It has been so many days. What are you waiting for? You want to kill me, right? Then kill me.'

'I will. On his thirty-sixth birthday. Till then you and I will stay here.'

'Why on his birthday? Why not now?'

'Old habits die hard,' the woman smiled.

'All right, I shall resign to what destiny has in store for me. I won't fight you. But I know that you have a lot to share which you perhaps have not shared with anyone before. Maybe, you never got a chance. I want to listen to you. I'm all ears to whatever it is that turned you into this . . . I asked you on the very first day itself and I'll ask you again, and I'll keep asking you this—who are you?' Prisha could tell that the woman was getting irritated. But it was her best bet to squeeze out more information from her.

The woman was sitting on the edge of the boat, sunning. She stood up and jumped down on the shore. Prisha could tell she hadn't gone very far because she could soon hear her sob.

'You there?' Prisha asked. She heard the sobs increase in intensity. Then suddenly the woman came back. And in a heavy, manly voice that sucked the air out of Prisha's lungs, she said, 'I'm his elder twin brother. Elder by a minute and thirty-seven seconds.'

'But Saveer told me his brother, Veer Rathod, is dead, just like his other family members. He never told me he had a twin brother,' Prisha said, realizing that her mouth had gone dry.

'He is a liar. He betrayed me and scarred me for the rest of my life.' She sat down opposite her.

Prisha could sense that she had hit the right nerve.

'You are right. I have never told my side of the story to anybody. It has now become like acid churning inside me. And acid corrodes even the vessel that contains it.'

A few minutes later, Prisha said softly, 'I'm listening.'

Eyes glistening with tears, the woman looked down at the floor, and drew her knees up against her chest and said, 'I am the elder one. My parents named me Saveer and my brother Veer. He was born a minute and thirty-seven seconds after me. But that's not the only difference between us. I was an early bloomer. I started speaking and walking before Veer; I started understanding things before him. Unfortunately, it worked against my favour. I was sharp. At the age of four, I understood why our uncle, Raghuveer Rathod, the so-called saint, visited us from his ashram. He didn't come to visit my family. He came to visit us: Veer and I. We aroused him. We, at the age of four! Can you believe how twisted and pathetic humans are? How filthy their fetishes can be? He used to sexually abuse me. He would touch me inappropriately and play with my genitals when nobody was looking. Though I was too young to understand sexual abuse, I did realize that he was doing something very wrong with me. Something I abhorred but could do nothing about. I told my parents that I hated my uncle, but they scolded me and told me to behave myself. I bit him once only to be slapped by my father.

'Then one day, I saw him doing the same with Veer. I thought it was my duty to protect my brother. I was always possessive about him; I cared for him. So from that day onwards, whenever Raghu uncle visited us, I would tell Veer to go hide himself. And when he called for him, I would go meet him as Veer. He couldn't guess. We were identical twins. I absorbed the abuse so my brother could be normal, be happy. But the experience changed me. I grew wild and unruly, becoming increasingly unmanageable, throwing tantrums, disobeying my parents. I turned anarchic and chaotic. So much so that my parents scolded and thrashed me almost every other day. I guess it was a reaction to not being heard.

'At the age of six, I again complained to my father about my uncle. He slapped me and my mother scolded me. They were getting concerned. I had grown increasingly aggressive and hyperactive over the past two years. They couldn't understand why, especially when Veer was normal and displayed no such mutinous behaviour. They decided to take me to a doctor and told my uncle about it. Seizing the opportunity, Raghu uncle made his abominable proposal. He convinced my parents that instead of a doctor, he was better suited to reforming my wayward ways. He said unchecked, I could grow up to tarnish the Rathods's reputation, bring a bad name to the family pedigree. *Bad name, huh!* He said I needed to be 'disciplined', 'reformed', not with medicines, but rather by staying with him in his ashram. That in the absence of my parents to give in to my tantrums, the austere life of the ashram might mend my ways. He said I would be returned to them in a few years. And my parents agreed!

'We are told that parents are living gods. But they are not. They are humans, who don't think twice before falling into the devil's trap. I was taken away; away from home, away from my parents, away from the one I loved the most: Veer. In his ashram, my uncle got a free hand to abuse me almost every other night. No one saw my tears, no one heard my cries. By that age, I knew that a man and a woman had sex to make babies. But I didn't understand why my uncle, a man, was fucking me, a boy. Did that mean that I was a woman? Who was I?' The woman paused. Prisha could almost picture the gut-wrenching scene of a small boy, pleading, crying helplessly as the devil himself trampled all over him.

'But, I soon 'reformed' my uncle. When I was ten, I hatched a plan against him. I decided to kill him. And I almost did. I caught a snake from a nearby zoo and left it in his chamber. I did this at the age of ten! Can you believe it?' she chuckled and continued, 'I planned the attack after faking my own death by burning a hut in the ashram. It was razed to the ground. No one suspected anything. One clever kid I was!' She laughed.

'After making sure that the snake had bitten my uncle, I ran back home. I could've gone back earlier after faking my death at the ashram, but who knew, maybe my parents would have sent me back and my uncle would have monitored and restricted my movements. I was happy, hopeful. I knew my parents would be shocked to see me alive. I wanted to tell them everything. I was certain that they would accept me with open arms.

'But what did I see upon returning? My brother was cutting his birthday cake. My parents were happy. They had forgotten me. Just like that! The brother for whom I had fucked up my own life, had erased me from his memory. How could people be so thankless? So selfish? So bloody greedy? It must not have been that long since I had left home, since I had been proclaimed dead. And my family was busy celebrating.

'Anyway, when I did muster courage and approached my father, he thought that I was the younger twin. Strangely, he addressed me as Saveer but believed that I was Veer. He behaved as if I had never really existed. I was stunned. I didn't understand why my brother, my little one, had never thought of correcting my parents. That he was Veer and not Saveer! But there was no place for me at home any more. My parents and my brother seemed to have wiped off all memories of me. Bitter and despairing, I ran away from home.

'Roaming around homeless, I nurtured an anger and hatred against Veer, the brother who had usurped my identity and had stolen my life. I swore to fuck his every happiness till I was alive. Till he was alive. It was then that I went on a killing spree. I killed my parents because

I hated them, was disgusted by their nonchalance, their insensitivity to come to my help, their refusal to listen to my complaints against my uncle, but more importantly, to let me go with him against my wishes, even while I cried myself hoarse, to not have made any attempts to contact me, to find out with me, to remember me.

'So I bred the Aedes Aegypti near our house and one of the mosquitoes bit my father and he contracted dengue. After his death, I racked my brains and came up with an even sinister plan to kill my mother. But I didn't even have to execute it. When I confronted her, years later, she was so shocked that soon after I left, she suffered a cardiac arrest. Maybe she realized that she had committed the most heinous sin ever by snatching the childhood away from a child.'

The woman stopped abruptly. Prisha tasted her own tears. She didn't know that she had started crying.

'You are not a woman for real? You are really his brother,' she said in a choked voice.

'Based on the genitalia an infant is born with, it is either declared a human male or a human female. But this is only one of our many identities. Years of constant sexual abuse had made me shudder at the thought of a man's touch. I couldn't see myself in the mirror. I couldn't see myself naked, you understand?' The woman sobbed.

'Imagine this: someone scars you so much at an impressionable age that you end up hating yourself. You hate the sex that you belong to. And it is so difficult to acknowledge that hatred, especially when you are born a male in a patriarchal society, when you are taught to take pride in your sex, when you are made to feel emasculated if don't perform the roles that have been ascribed to men. The most primitive war is between the penis and the vagina. And it has seeped into our system so much that it doesn't even seem like a war any more. It was meant to complement each other and take life forward but we ended up pronouncing one's strength and declaring the other, the weaker sex.

'My only blessing was that I was sharp and could therefore find work. The day I turned twenty-one, I underwent a sex-change operation in Bangkok. I had worked hard and collected enough money by doing odd jobs. I killed the man in me. I felt happy to be a woman. I felt alive after a long time. Suddenly, it didn't seem like I had the body which had been preyed upon. Suddenly, I felt sacred from within. But then I realized, it is even more difficult to be a woman. A man can only be fucked by other men. But a woman is constantly gang-banged by both men and the society. But I survived. Somehow.'

But the woman soon sounded bitter. 'The happiness was nothing in comparison to the hatred I felt for Veer. My uncle had only manipulated my parents, but he had manipulated everybody by becoming Saveer. That little bastard whom I loved and cared for so much . . .

for whom I had sacrificed my own self,' she spat on the ground.

The *real* Saveer then went outside. Prisha didn't know what to think, what to say or what to feel. For the first time since she had been kidnapped, she did not think about her freedom. She had always thought that the murderer, whoever he was, had to be a psycho, but she wasn't so sure any more. We all build our own prisons, sketch our own version of hell and choose to live our whole life assuming there isn't more to either the prison or the hell. What Saveer—the real one—needed was freedom, not revenge. It was evident he had mistaken one for the other.

Prisha didn't eat or sleep that day. Saveer came back late at night and lay down next to Prisha.

'Do you know what your biggest problem is?' Prisha asked. There was no response but she knew that Saveer was listening to her.

'It's not your past. Not even what happened to you. Of course, god forbid such a heinous and dastardly thing from happening to any child, or to anyone for that matter, but it had all happened years ago. Your biggest problem is that you are obsessed with your brother and his happiness. In that obsession, you've forgotten that you're actually free. And that's your only and biggest problem. You have forgotten to live freely. You said you would kill me on his thirty-sixth birthday. But what after that? You know this very well that he won't involve himself with anybody after my death. Neither will he have a purpose in his life nor will you. You tell me, where do you and your life figure in all this? Shit happens to a lot of people. I agree, in your case it was as ugly as it could be, but does that mean you don't deserve to live the way you should? With dignity, with freedom, without making one individual the purpose of your life? You tattooed on his back that you will fuck his every happiness, but honestly, I feel that you have fucked up your happiness the most in all these years. He had Ishanvi, he had me. But who did you have? Did you even give anyone a chance? What I know about love is that it can be both a whiplash and a healer. Depends on how we let it affect us. I know you are listening to me, so speak up. Damn it!'

Prisha was right. Every word of hers had been consumed. The woman turned to face her.

'Come to the point,' she said.

'The point is simple. If you still feel that imprisoning me here and then killing me on his birthday will solve anything then you are delusional. If someone, years ago, destroyed something as beautiful as your childhood, then now, years later, you too are doing the same. You are destroying a beautiful life which I can have, which he can have and which you too can have.'

'Come to the point,' the woman repeated herself.

Prisha took a deep breath. It was time to say what she had on her mind.

'You allow me to go. I will call up the police and tell them where I am. They will come fetch me. I will feed them a false story, say that I don't know who my abductor was or what he looked like. I'll tell them that I somehow managed to escape. I won't tell them anything—not even that you are a woman now. And that frees you for life. You may have killed people. In fact, you killed my friend too. But I now know this for a fact that you are *not* a killer. You are *not* a murderer. *You are not your uncle.*'

Saveer blinked, tears rolled down her cheeks. They kept looking at each other. After a while, Prisha said, 'You hold the guy I love the most responsible for your unhappiness. Have you ever tried to know his version of the story? Maybe he was not the one who betrayed you. Maybe he had been fed a wrong story. Did you ever give him a chance to explain? Did you? All hell had broken loose on him for all these years. He is your brother, after all! Your little one! What if you came to know that he had been innocent all along? Won't it destroy you as badly as your uncle had destroyed you?'

Each and every word was an unexpected punch. The woman had not expected a young girl like Prisha to have interpreted her story in a way that she herself had never thought of. It was as if till now her life had been one long running sentence and Prisha had just told her that it was high time she put a full stop. And a change of paragraph didn't mean an end to the story. It meant another beginning. *Do I really have a life beyond this complicated mess that I have created for myself and others?* she thought. She could smell freedom in the thought which Prisha's words had created in her. And a soul, caged inside its own dark thoughts, can't be imprisoned any more after it had sniffed the scent of freedom. She turned and blew out the flame in the lantern—the only source of light in the boat.

29

On the thirteenth day of Prisha's disappearance, Saveer got a call from an unknown number. He had not had a wink of sleep in the last thirteen days. He picked it up after the third ring. His heart raced, hearing Prisha's distressed voice. She told him she was calling from a PCO in a village near Bengaluru. Saveer, who was with Shetty at that time, put her on speaker. Shetty jotted down the details of the location and passed it on to his team. Prisha was asked to stay where she was. After the lead given by the courier company's guard, the police had considered that Prisha could be in Mandya but had failed to trace her. She was finally tracked down after two hours. Saveer, Gauri and her parents accompanied the police to the village.

Prisha and her parents broke down when they met each other. She looked weak and fragile. Gauri sobbed while hugging her.

'You almost killed me, bro.' she said.

'Tell me about it,' Prisha said and looked across at Saveer. Standing right behind her parents, he felt like a curse had been lifted from him. They neither hugged nor shook hands.

The police wanted a statement from Prisha. She directed them to the boat where she had been kept as a captive. She told them it was never a woman but a man. Saveer's twin brother, Veer. He was there with her for twelve days, after which he didn't come back. Prisha managed to call for help and was rescued by some locals. She also mentioned that Veer did not torture or harass her during the time he held her in captivity. The police continued their search for a few more days but they couldn't track Veer Rathod. On Prisha's request, Saveer asked Shetty to close the case.

'He didn't tell me if every death was a coincidence or not, but he confessed to having pushed me off the hill,' Prisha told Shetty in her statement. Her over-defensive stand raised his suspicion but he had no lead to prove otherwise.

'What about Diggy?' Saveer asked.

'He wasn't involved. That was someone else. At least that's what he told me. I don't think he had any reason to lie to me at least,' she said. Saveer did not have any reason to doubt her. Through all her lies, Prisha knew that she was setting someone else's life right.

Prisha was staying with her parents in a hotel. Though she had convinced her parents once again to let her stay back in Bengaluru for her studies, her father couldn't digest the fact that her boyfriend was double her age. And that she had faced serious, life threatening danger because of him—twice.

'It's all over now, Papa. Nothing bad will happen again,' she assured him. They were in the hotel room. Prisha knew that she needed to be more convincing. But she had a lot of time to do that. Seeing her family happy, Prisha remembered the real Saveer's story. There were parents out there who were responsible for destroying their own children's lives. Prisha felt lucky to have parents who had always supported her dreams and aspirations. It was both an experience and a lesson for life. Never in her wildest imagination could she ever feel what the real Saveer must have gone through. She cried many a time under the shower recalling the story but promised herself to not reveal it to anybody no matter what. Not even to her Saveer.

As she came out of the shower, she received a message on her new phone: *I'm at the lobby*. Prisha excused herself and went downstairs. Saveer was waiting for her. She hugged him tight.

'I thought I had lost *us*,' Prisha said.

'You thought? I was sure.'

Prisha broke the hug and said, 'Didn't you know your brother was alive? And that he was your twin?'

'No! I was pretty young when it had all happened.'

Prisha was happy to know that his version matched the story she had heard days ago from the real Saveer. Even then, she felt sorry for him—his parents had lied to him about his own brother.

'But I realized something.' Saveer said, 'I used to look for him everywhere after he was gone but my parents convinced me that there had been nobody. When I told them I had seen someone resembling me before and he wasn't there any more, my parents said I used to look at my own reflection in the mirror. I simply couldn't guess that I had a twin brother. I was just four or five at that time for heaven's sake.'

Someone else was also four or five then. And he had been subjected to hell.

'What I never understood was why my parents would lie to me about him?'

You may not know ever, but I do. And I also know that you are Veer, the younger one. The little one, Prisha thought. She was tempted to ask how he had become Saveer from Veer, but knew he would probably not have an answer to that. His parents were dead, and that part of the story had gone with them. All that remained was a sibling saga in which one brother had misinterpreted the story and the other was misinformed. Hadn't the real Saveer mentioned that he would often pretend to be Veer? Could it be that that confusion had persisted? Was it possible for the mother to have not been able to distinguish between her sons? Did they think it was Veer who was becoming wilder by the day? Did the uncle think that it was Veer whom he was taking away? Did the parents never realize their mistake? But why didn't Veer himself correct them as Saveer had pointed out? Or did he simply abide by what his brother had taught him: to pretend to be him? Who knows? Prisha realized that neither she nor Saveer or Veer would ever get to know the truth. Maybe it was time to move on and let bygones be bygones.

'Listen, I want you to join my parents for dinner tomorrow. Not as my professor. But as my future . . .'

'Future?'

'Life partner. They don't get the concept of a double-my-age boyfriend.'

'And what about life partner then? Are they okay with that?'

'We will see. They are old school. If there's anything they will be okay with, it would be a life partner.'

They smiled at each other.

'Just remember, don't look your usual sexy self,' Prisha said with a straight face.

'Yeah?'

'Yeah. I don't want my parents to know that their daughter has become a horny bitch staying alone here.'

Saveer laughed hard, feeling happy after a long time. What he didn't know was that someone somewhere didn't have a problem with him being happy any more.

30

Months later
Saveer's thirty-sixth birthday

The alarm woke him up. He had set it for 12 a.m. It was his birthday. And before Prisha could surprise him, he hoped to tell her straightaway that he only wanted her by his side. Not any surprise. He had got his fair share of surprises already. Now he wanted to be certain about everything. After all, his life wasn't his any more. Life was *theirs*. Their individual journeys may have been different, but now they had come together. It was one road from here onwards. The sun would be theirs and so would be the shade. The complaints, the mistakes, the lessons, the realizations and the happiness . . . they would share everything. Saveer and Prisha had got engaged a month ago. It had been difficult convincing Prisha's parents, and they accepted him only after he had slipped a ring on Prisha's finger. They would get married a few years later.

Saveer tried opening his eyes but realized that he had been blindfolded. He immediately got alarmed and tried taking it off but realized that he was handcuffed to the bed. His legs were tied as well. He was only in his boxers. Saveer was about to shout for help when he felt something ghastly cold on his right foot. He squirmed and goosebumps appeared on his leg.

'Prisha, is that you?' he asked loudly and then realized it couldn't have been her since the house was locked and she did not have any spare key. He was about say something else when he felt something warm on his left foot. As if someone was holding a flame above it. The coldness and the warmth together started climbing up his legs as Saveer fidgeted on the bed helplessly. In the midst of all the confusion, he couldn't help but feel aroused. There was the sound of muffled laughter. The coldness had travelled all the up to his inner thighs and was dangerously close to his shorts.

'Whoever you are . . . fuck you!' Saveer said, unable to take it any more. He already had an aching hard on.

'Promise, Monster?' Prisha asked. Saveer's lips stretched into a grin.

'Girl, you are gone!' he said.

'You'll have your chance. Right now it's mine,' she said, hovering the ice cube and the lighter above his thighs. She loved the way his penis was poking his shorts. She kept the lighter and the ice cube aside and kissed his thighs.

'I hope by now you have realized that you have made a Mean Monster out of me,' Prisha said in a naughty voice.

'Uh huh! go ahead, show me how good a student you have been,' Saveer said in a raspy voice. He felt his shorts being tugged down to his knees. The way she pressed at different points on his erect shaft while her tongue slurped on his balls made him clench his fist in ecstasy.

'You really going to do this to me, baby?' he pleaded. He heard her laugh.

'You want me to stuff your mouth as well?' she asked and crept up. He had his mouth open, expecting a kiss. It was a slurpy smooch. The way she sucked his tongue, sometimes urgently and at times gently, it seemed she was trying to call out to his soul. She slowly sat down on his erect penis, pushing it inside her wet vagina. Prisha started with slow hip movements and then closed her eyes. It had been long since they had been this intimate. Everything, right from the beginning, started flashing before her eyes. From the time she had seen him at Zinnia's place to the moment she had hugged him in the hotel lobby, Gauri and her parents. Her long moans were punctuated by his fierce grunts. It only made her ride him harder. With him, she had understood that an orgasm was like a perfect world. And she could feel that she was about to enter that world. She came soon. And did so crying his name out loud and digging her nails into his chest. He was her *territory* now. Period. She'd claimed him after a long war. And no power would be able to steal him from her.

Panting, she collapsed on him, breathing close to his mouth. With one hand, she removed his blindfold. Her hair veiled his face. Prisha unlocked the handcuffs. He immediately put his arms around her.

'Happy birthday, love,' she smiled.

'Thanks. But you scared me at first,' he whispered. Their eyes were fixed on each other.

'I'm sorry but I had to do this,' she whispered back.

'I never thought I will have a normal birthday, ever.'

'From now onwards you will.'

'Do you think he will come back?'

'No, he won't.'

Saveer was surprised at her confidence.

'How do you know?' he asked.

'If he had to return, he wouldn't have left,' she said.

'Hmm. I wonder what made him change his mind. Why did he leave you and spare me after so many years?'

You can be a slave to your own demons for years but to be free, you need just a moment, Prisha thought.

'By the way, how did you get the keys?'

For a moment, Prisha averted her eyes.

'I was planning this for some time. Made a duplicate one,' she lied. She had secured the duplicate key from the boat after the real Saveer had left. In her heart, however, Prisha knew this lie would save someone. Someone who had suffered enough. Someone who deserved to be free.

She'd promised *her* it would be their secret. And she would keep her promise till her last breath.

'Hmm,' Saveer looked deeply into her eyes. Their lips were barely apart from each other. For some time, neither spoke a word.

'I lo . . .' Saveer started but she put her hand over his mouth. 'Don't say it. Someone had once told me that if you say everything you lose the magic.'

'Really?' he smiled, 'Who's that someone?'

This time Prisha looked deeply into his eyes.

'He is my soul-tattoo . . . my *forever*,' Prisha said and placing her ear on his chest, listened to his heartbeats. They were telling her their story—the past, the present and the future.

Epilogue

Place: A budget hotel
Date: 9 November
Time: 11.30 p.m.

She drew all the curtains in the room and switched off all the unnecessary lights, letting only an old lamp burn in a corner.

In the warm glow of the lamp, she saw the reflection of her body in the mirror. She could see a woman; it made her feel at peace with herself.

She opened her bag and took out the things she had bought from a nearby store. Mostly essentials except for one thing. She took it out and kept it on the not-very-clean glass top of a discoloured centre table. She had bought it for the first time in her life. A birthday cake. Nothing fancy. And yet it filled her with an unprecedented joy. She carefully stuck a small candle in it and lit it with a matchstick.

'Happy birthday,' she wished herself, not remembering the last time she had heard herself say so. *Prisha was right,* she thought. That obsession which yields nothing but hatred destroys oneself in the end. True, it isn't a perfect world. Perfect things are only there in our hearts. And the moment we move out of our comfort zones, we expose ourselves to the risk of being altered by situations. And people. There are moments when we can't do much and become victims and then there are instances when we fight back. But rarely do we appreciate the power of our minds. It can heal us if we allow it to. And burn us if we let it. Had it not been for Prisha, she wouldn't have known that she could still smile without a reason. Just by looking at a small birthday cake. And if one can do that, one can be rest assured of living life just for oneself.

She took a deep breath. Suddenly the purpose of seeking her happiness seemed way bigger than screwing her brother's. In the end, all of us will turn into ashes or be buried deep inside the earth. Then why not make the journey till then as fulfilling as possible?

She smiled looking at the candle on top of the cake. *After a long time, it was the moment to celebrate life*, she thought, and blew out the candle in one breath. With that several other lights lit up in her. And in those lights she finally knew who she was.

Acknowledgments

My heartfelt thanks and deep gratitude to Milee Ashwarya for her continuous faith in my storytelling prowess and fruitful support as a publisher.

My editor Indrani, publicist Shruti, Peter and the entire digital and sales team at Penguin Random House for working hard and helping my vision reach the readers smoothly every time.

Deeply grateful to my family for their continuous support and understanding which allows me to do what I love doing the most.

Anmol and Likhith: thanks for all your help, support and love.

Special thanks: Ranisa, Whoosh.

R—always, in all ways.

About the Author

Novoneel Chakraborty is the bestselling author of ten romantic thriller novels. His novel *Forget Me Not, Stranger* debuted as the No. 1 bestseller across India, while the second in the Stranger series, *All Yours, Stranger*, ranked among the top five thriller novels on Amazon, India. *Black Suits You* also ranked among the top five thrillers on Amazon for fifteen weeks straight.

Known for his twists, dark plots and strong female protagonists, Novoneel is referred to as the Sidney Sheldon of India by his readers.

Apart from novels, Novoneel has written seven TV shows. He lives and works in Mumbai.

You can get in touch with him at:

Email: novosphere@gmail.com
Facebook: officialnbc
Twitter: @novoxeno
Instagram: @novoneelchakraborty
Blog: www.nbconline.blogspot.com

ALSO BY THE SAME AUTHOR

Forever Is a Lie

The best thing happened to her, but in the worst way possible . . .

Eighteen-year-old Prisha Srivastav is a student of mass communication in Bengaluru. She meets a mysterious man, almost double her age, known as the 'Mean Monster' in the city's party circuit. Intrigued, she falls for him and pursues him. However, there is one problem. Prisha doesn't know that whoever the Monster loves, dies.

From the master of twists, Novoneel Chakraborty, comes yet another beguiling tale of dark romance and thrill that won't let you put the book down.